L.M. Montgomery's

Anne of
Green Gables

C000053563

adapted by

Sylvia Ashby

Baker's Plays
7611 Sunset Blvd.
Los Angeles, CA 90046
bakersplays.com

FOR

my mother and foster mother, in memory

and

my husband, who brought this script to life

ABOUT THE PLAY

The action of this adaptation is continuous, one scene blending into another. The passage of time is conveyed through words, movement, costumes, and lighting. None of these elements should interrupt the continuity: As the dialogue in one scene ends, dialogue in the following scene begins. No music is needed for transitions. A quick cross-fade will suffice when lighting changes are required. The "Lights Up" cues in the script are intended to focus the attention of the reader rather than supply directions for the designer.

This script, which should be performed at a brisk pace, runs a few minutes over two hours, excluding intermission. There are sixteen roles, nine women, seven men; some doubling is possible. Production Notes, at the back of the script, include an alternate--boatless--version of the "Playing Camelot" scene.

ANNE OF GREEN GABLES was first presented in October, 1990 at the Lubbock Community Theatre (Lubbock, TX) under the direction of Cliff Ashby, with the following cast:

Anne Shirley . . . . Ali Selim
Marilla Cuthbert . . . . Linda Huckabee
Mathew Cuthbert . . . . Harlan Reddell
Rachel Lynde . . . . Karen Copple
Station Master . . . . Tom Copple
Mr. Spencer . . . . Bill Lanier
Mrs. Blewitt . . . . Susan Andrews
Diana Barry . . . . Jamie Boylan
Mrs. Barry . . . . Mickie Klafka
Mr. Phillips . . . . Mack Yates
Miss Stacy . . . . Lucette Sheppard
Ruby Gillis . . . . Amber Orr
Josie Pye . . . . Alayna Roberts
Moody MacPherson . . . . Chad Miller
Charlie Sloane . . . . Sam Patton
Gilbert Blythe . . . . Andy Hutton

Assistant Director/Stage Manager . . . . Cynthia Kent

The play was subsequently produced by Columbia Entertainment Company, Columbia, MO.; Escola Maria Imaculada, Sao Paulo, Brazil; Garza Theatre, Post, TX.

CHARACTERS

ANNE SHIRLEY, a young orphan about 12 1/2
MARILLA CUTHBERT, a middle-aged spinster
MATHEW CUTHBERT, her bachelor brother
RACHEL LYNDE, a neighbor
STATION MASTER, at Bright River
MR. SPENCER, from a nearby village
MRS. BLEWITT, his neighbor
DIANA BARRY, Anne's friend
MRS. BARRY, Diana's mother
MR. PHILLIPS, Avonlea teacher
MISS STACY, new teacher
RUBY GILLIS, schoolmate
JOSIE PYE, schoolmate
MOODY MACPHERSON, schoolmate
CHARLIE SLOANE, schoolmate
GILBERT BLYTHE, schoolmate

TIME AND PLACE
Early 1900's, Prince Edward Island, Canada. Action covers a period of four years.

SETTING
Cuthbert farmhouse in Avonlea. The downstage space is flexible, transforming into various locales.

ANNE OF GREEN GABLES

(*Setting: Two rooms of the Cuthbert farmhouse. The bedroom is Stage Left, the kitchen is Stage Right. The kitchen leads to the hall and pantry. The set is fragmentary and suggestive. The Downstage area is flexible, becoming various locales. Down Right is a bench or platform seat. No pantomime of opening doors and windows is needed. RACHEL enters Right, sweeping. She glances up.*)

RACHEL: As I live and breathe! Mathew Cuthbert! In his Sunday suit! On a week day! Where's he going and why? That's what I'd like to know. Doesn't need his Sunday suit to go after turnip seed. And he wasn't driving fast enough to go for the doctor. (*Prim and middle-aged, MARILLA enters kitchen, sets table.*) I'm clean puzzled and won't know a moment's peace till I ask Marilla. (*Crossing*) If you want my opinion--which I'm sure you don't--that brother of hers is the oddest fellow in all Canada! Can't get a blessed word out of him. Marilla!

MARILLA: Come in, Rachel. (*To Audience*) I knew she'd be right over.

RACHEL: (*To Audience*) Hmmm. . . three plates. . . must be expecting company. But everyday dishes? (*Marilla offers rocker*) Believe I will set a spell!

MARILLA: (*Suppressing a smile*) Fine evening, isn't it?

RACHEL: (*Fidgets, bursting with curiosity*) Fine. Fine.

MARILLA: (*Toys with Rachel*) How's the family?

RACHEL: Fine. Fine. (*Rocks nervously, then:*) Marilla Cuthbert! Where--for heaven's sake--was Mathew going in that buggy?

MARILLA: (*To Audience*) Thought she'd never ask. (*Turns*) Mathew went down to the station at Bright River. We're getting a young boy from the orphan asylum in Nova Scotia.

RACHEL: Marilla Cuthbert, I think you're actually serious!

MARILLA: Of course. The boy's coming in on the train.

RACHEL: (*To Audience*) Adopting a boy! An old maid and a bachelor!

(*LIGHTS UP LEFT: Simultaneous Scenes. A twelve-year old girl enters with worn suitcase.*)

ANNE: My arms are black and blue from pinching myself. So I can't be dreaming. It's real: I am going to live on Prince Edward Island! With a family of my very own! Maybe even a bosom friend! (*Sits on suitcase*)

RACHEL: Marilla, what on earth put such a notion into your head?

MARILLA: We've been thinking it over a while. Spencers were getting a five-year old girl from the asylum and knew all about it. But Mathew and I decided to take a boy--about twelve or so.

RACHEL: Nothing will ever surprise me again. Nothing.

MARILLA: Mathew's getting up in years. His heart troubles him now and again. And finding reliable help is near to impossible.

RACHEL: Lord, isn't that the awful truth! If you want

my opinion--

MARILLA: (*Interrupts*) When we heard Mr. Spencer was picking up their girl, we sent word for him to bring us a nice Canadian lad. Old enough to be useful and young enough to be brought up proper.

ANNE: If no one comes tonight--I'll stay in that wild cherry tree--all white with bloom in the moonlight. . . and pretend I'm with one of my make-believe friends.

RACHEL: (*Rises*) Marilla, you're doing a mighty foolish thing bringing a strange child into your home. Last week I read of a couple took in an orphan boy and he set fire to the house--on purpose, Marilla! Nearly burned them to a crisp in their beds.

MARILLA: I don't deny I've had some qualms.

RACHEL: Another adopted boy used to *suck eggs*! They couldn't break him of it, no way! (*At door*) Well, if you'd asked my opinion--which you *didn't*--I'd have said, "Gracious sakes, don't do such a thing!"

MARILLA: Mathew was terrible set on it so I gave in. It's seldom he fixes his mind on anything.

RACHEL: (*Coming back*) And I just heard of a case in New Brunswick where an asylum child put strychnine in the well--whole family died in fearful agonies. Only it was a girl in that instance.

MARILLA: We're not getting a girl. Fact is, I wonder at Mrs. Spencer for trying it. I'd never dream of taking a girl to bring up.

RACHEL: Don't say I didn't warn you. (*Outside:*) Poor lad! What those two know about children wouldn't fill a thimble. Well, I'm on my way to the MacPhersons. This will make a sensation! (*FADE*)

(LIGHTS UP LEFT: A shy, inarticulate GENTLEMAN enters; looking about, HE passes an expectant ANNE. STATION MASTER enters quickly.)

STATION MASTER: (*Friendly*)   Oh, Mr. Cuthbert! Good evening to you, Sir.

MATHEW: I suppose the five-thirty train will be along soon.

STATION MASTER: Nope.   (*Checks watch*)   The five-thirty's been and gone--half an hour ago.

MATHEW: (*Distressed*)   But--I am expecting--a little--

STATION MASTER: A little girl. Yes--she's sitting right there. I invited her to the waiting room but the child prefers to stay outside. "More scope for the imagination," she says.

MATHEW: (*Confused*)   It's a boy I've come for.   Mr. Alexander Spencer was to bring a boy over--from Nova Scotia.

STATION MASTER: Mr. Spencer stepped off the train with that girl.   Said you'd be along presently.   Course, he was going on to White Sands station. I'm on my way home for supper--

MATHEW: (*Still bewildered*)   A boy is--is what we asked for.

STATION MASTER: Sorry, Mr. Cuthbert.   There's only one orphan on the premises.

MATHEW: I don't understand.   (*To Audience*)   I wish Marilla was here now.

STATION MASTER: Maybe they were out of the brand of boy you wanted!   But she can explain--that young one's got a tongue on her.   (*Exits*)

MATHEW: I can't ask her why she's not a boy. Or tell her there's some mistake.   Can't just leave her at the station. Best take the child home for now.   (*Relief*) And let Marilla do the explaining! (*MATHEW approaches in terror. ANNE leaps up.*)

ANNE: (*Shaking his hand*) I suppose you are Mathew Cuthbert of Green Gables? I'm glad to meet you. I was afraid I might have to sleep in that cherry tree.

MATHEW: (*Painfully shy*) I'm. . . sorry I'm late.

ANNE: It seems so wonderful that I'm going to live with you. I've never belonged to anybody--not really.

MATHEW: I'll--I'll take your suitcase, Miss. Buggy's over yonder.

ANNE: Oh, I can manage--not very heavy. Though it contains all my worldly goods and chattels. What are chattels anyway?

MATHEW: Can't say as I know. (*Crossing Center, ANNE sets down suitcase for "Buggy" seat.*)

MATHEW: (*"Helping" her*) Step right in, Miss.

ANNE: (*Sits*) Think of all there is to find out! Makes me glad to be alive--in such an interesting world.

MATHEW: (*Yanks "reins"*) Get a move on, Pearl. (*THEY mime travel; clip-clop SOUND of horse FADES gradually.*)

ANNE: I just love riding. . . . Mr. Cuthbert, what do those white lacy blossoms remind you of?

MATHEW: Well now, I dunno. . . .

ANNE: A bride maybe--with a misty veil. But nobody would ever marry me--except a foreign missionary who couldn't be too particular.

MATHEW: Well now. . . I wouldn't say that. . . .

ANNE: Though I'd love to have a dress with great puffed sleeves. Never had a pretty dress--that I can remember. So it's more to look forward to, isn't it?

MATHEW: Well now. . . I suppose it is.

ANNE: (*Rattling*) Am I talking too much? People always

tell me I do. I can stop when I decide to, although it's *very* difficult.

MATHEW: Talk as much as you like. I don't mind. (*To Audience, surprised*) Truth is, I sort of like her chatter.

ANNE: You and I are going to be kindred spirits. *Indubit-ably.* (*Mathew glances*) People laugh at me for using big words. But if you have big ideas, you need big words to express them.

MATHEW: (*Enjoying himself*) Well now. . . that sounds reasonable enough.

ANNE: Right now I feel almost perfectly happy. I can't feel totally perfectly happy because--well--what color would you call this? (*Holds out braid*)

MATHEW: It's red, ain't it?

ANNE: Nobody with red hair can be perfectly happy. The freckles--the green eyes--I can imagine them away. But I cannot imagine red hair away. (*Tragic*) It will be my lifelong sorrow.

MATHEW: Well, I dunno 'bout that.

ANNE: (*Suddenly awestruck*) Oh Mr. Cuthbert!   Mr. Cuthbert!

MATHEW: (*Stops*) Whooooaa, Pearl. (*Explains*) They call it The Avenue.

ANNE: How poetical. Riding under a canopy of apple blossoms!

MATHEW: Right pretty place--The Avenue.

ANNE: They should call it--White Way of Delight!

MATHEW: Well now, that's a fine name!   Never would've thought of that.

ANNE: I always name the things I love.

MATHEW: (*Starting up*) We're coming pretty near home now.

ANNE: Home!   To think of coming to a real home--
(*Jumps up, pointing*) Oh Mr. Cuthbert!

MATHEW: (*Explains again*) Barry's Pond.

ANNE: I shall name it--Lake of Shining Waters! (*Tumbles back with jolt*)

MATHEW: Guess "Barry's Pond" is a mite plain--and--a--

ANNE: Sensible?

MATHEW: That's the word!   And here's Green Gables right over this hill.

ANNE: I'm going to shut my eyes tight.   (*Slowly opens eyes, momentarily speechless as buggy halts*)   Oh--it's like a dream. . . .   (*While dread overtakes Mathew, ANNE joyfully darts Left.*)   I can hear a brook running--listen to the trees talking-- (*MATHEW stands motionless*) Are you coming?

MATHEW: (*To Audience*) I'm afraid so. (*Crosses*) This way. (*ANNE follows with suitcase; MATHEW ushers her in.*)

MARILLA: (*Enters, looking around*) Mathew! Where is the boy?

MATHEW: (*Glumly*) There is no boy. Only her.

MARILLA: There must be--we sent word for Mr. Spencer to bring us a boy.

MATHEW: Well, he didn't. Mr. Spencer only delivered a girl.

MARILLA: Mercy sakes!

MATHEW: Had to bring the child home. Couldn't leave her at the station--no matter where the mistake come in.

MARILLA: This is a fine kettle of fish!

ANNE: You don't want me. Because I'm not a boy. I might have expected it.   I might have known it was too beautiful to last. (*Flings herself into rocker, weeping*)

MARILLA: (*Taken aback*) Is she plum daft or what?

MATHEW: Well. . . no. . . not--exactly.

MARILLA: And what am I supposed to do?

MATHEW: (*Miserable*) Don't rightly know. . . . (*Sits*)

MARILLA: (*Lamely*) Child, there's no need to take on so.

ANNE: You'd cry too if you were an orphan arriving some place you thought was home--only to discover they didn't want you either. (*Dramatic*) Oh, this is the most *tragical* event of my whole life!

MARILLA: Don't get in a fever over it. We're not going to turn you out--tonight. What is your name, child?

ANNE: Will you please call me Cordelia?

MARILLA: Call you Cordelia? Is that your name?

ANNE: Not precisely. But Cordelia is such a perfectly elegant name.

MARILLA: Whatever do you mean? If Cordelia isn't your name, what is?

ANNE: Anne Shirley! But please call me Cordelia. Anne is such an unromantic name.

MARILLA: Fiddlesticks! Anne is a good plain--*sensible* name.

ANNE: I used to pretend I was Geraldine but I prefer Cordelia now. If you must call me Anne, please call me Anne spelled with an E.

MARILLA: (*Pours tea*) What difference does it make how it's spelled?

ANNE: Simple old A-N-N looks dreadful. But A-N-N-E looks ever so much more distinguished.

MARILLA: Very well then, Anne spelled with an E, can you tell us how this mistake came to be made. Were no boys available?

ANNE: An abundance. But *Mrs*. Spencer said you distinctly wanted a girl--about my age. Manager thought I would do. Couldn't sleep a wink all night--I was so thrilled.

MARILLA: (*Mutters*) Never should have trusted that Mabel Spencer to--

ANNE: (*Springs up, accusing*) Why didn't you just leave me at the station! Wish I'd never seen White Way of Delight-- Lake of Shining Waters-- (*Slumps back*)

MARILLA: What on earth is she talking about!

MATHEW: Er-uh--she's just referring to some conversation--we had on the way over-- (*Nervously gulps tea*)

MARILLA: Sit down to supper. Did Mr. Spencer bring over anybody else?

ANNE: Just Lily Jones--for himself. (*Sits*) If I was five years old with beautiful nut-brown hair, would you keep me?

MARILLA: We want a boy on the farm. A girl would be of no use.

MATHEW: You're not eating . . . .

ANNE: Can you eat when you're in the depths of despair?

MARILLA: I've never been in the "depths of despair," so I can't say.

ANNE: (*Soulful*) "My life is a graveyard of buried hopes."

MARILLA: What!

ANNE: I say that to comfort myself.

MARILLA: Don't see where the comfort comes in.

ANNE: Just a sentence from a book. The heroine says it three times.

MARILLA: I was never allowed to read such foolishness.

MATHEW: (*Uneasy*) I guess she's tired. Best put her to bed, Marilla.

MARILLA: (*Crosses to bedroom*) Come along, child. This is where you sleep--for *tonight*. (*Anne carries suitcase to closet*) Undress quick and go to bed. I suppose you have a nightgown.

ANNE: Just old flannel--but I pretend it's flowing silk--

MARILLA: It's sinful to think about clothes too much. Good night, Anne.

ANNE: (*Alone*) *Good* night? This is the very worst night of my whole life! (*Throws herself on bed, quietly sobbing*)

MARILLA: (*Clears table, slamming plates*) Well, this is a pretty piece of business! First thing tomorrow, I'll send word to Mr. Spencer. That girl goes back to the asylum.

MATHEW: (*Downcast*) Yes, I suppose so. . . .

MARILLA: You suppose so! Don't you know?

MATHEW: Well now, she's a real nice little thing, Marilla. Kind of a pity to send her back when she's so set on staying.

MARILLA: Mathew Cuthbert! You mean to say we ought to keep her!

MATHEW: (*Stammers*) Well now, no--I suppose not--not exactly. I--I--suppose--we could--hardly be expected to--

MARILLA: I should say not. What good would she be to us?

MATHEW: Well-- (*Blurting*) We might be of some good to her!

MARILLA: Mathew Cuthbert, I believe the child has bewitched you. I can see--plain as plain--you want to keep that urchin!

MATHEW: She's such an interesting little person, Marilla. You should have heard her talk coming from the station.

MARILLA: It's nothing in her favor either--unless you're as odd as she is!

MATHEW: Well, maybe I am! Cause--I--I kind of like her meanderings.

MARILLA: I don't want an orphan *girl*. If I did, she's not the style I fancy. The child goes straight back to where she came from.

MATHEW: I could hire a farm boy to help. The girl'd be company for you.

MARILLA: (*Untying apron*) I'm not suffering for company. Tomorrow, Mr. Spencer can come fetch her. Good night, Mathew. (*Exits*)

MATHEW: Well now, it's--just as you say, Marilla. (*Follows, resigned. Still in dress, ANNE springs from her bed.*)

ANNE: By morning I wasn't in the depths of despair anymore. That's why mornings are splendid!   From my window I heard the brook laughing--saw the orchard blooming as if it meant it. And I made up my mind to enjoy this day, no matter what! (*ANNE marches to kitchen; MARILLA washes dishes.*) This morning I imagined I was a a bee living in an apple blossom. Wouldn't it be wonderful if flowers could talk?

MARILLA: There's enough talk around here already.

ANNE: Then I caught a glimpse of the sea and imagined I was a gull swooping down. (*Swoops around kitchen*)

MARILLA: (*Presents towel*) Can you imagine doing the dishes? That's more to the point.

ANNE: I'm better at looking after children--too bad you don't have any.

MARILLA: I have more than I need for the present, thank you.

ANNE: (*Drying*) Mrs. Hammond had eight--twins three times in succession is too much. And I told her so when the last pair came!

MARILLA: As you're bent on talking, tell me what you know about yourself.

ANNE: I used to imagine I was a princess stolen away by an evil nurse who died before she could confess the truth.

MARILLA: Just stick to the bald facts, if you please.

ANNE: (*Relents*) Well, after my folks died of the fever, nobody really wanted me. So Mrs. Thomas took me in--said I was the homeliest, scrawniest child. Stayed till I was eight, looking after children. But Mr. Thomas got drunk once too often--was killed falling under a train--so Mrs. Thomas moved back home.

MARILLA: (*Dazed*) I don't think I'm following all this.

ANNE: Very simple: Her folks didn't want me either. That's when Mrs. Hammond said she'd take me, seeing I was handy with children.

MARILLA: Then how did you come to be at the asylum?

ANNE: After Mrs. Hammond's husband ran off, she parceled out the twins and shipped me to the asylum.

MARILLA: Were they--good to you--these women?

ANNE: Oh, they meant to be. Of course, the asylum was full up so they didn't want me. But I stayed three months--till Mr. Spencer came.

MARILLA: (*Glances out*) Well, he's coming for you now. Get your things. (*Crosses to yard*) And who's that with him? Mrs. Blewitt! That stingy, mean-tempered-- (*MR. SPENCER enters Left with MRS. BLEWITT, who stands, glaring.*)

MR. SPENCER: (*Crosses, anxious*) Hello, Miss Cuthbert. And how are you, Anne?

ANNE: (*Gloomily returns with suitcase*) As well as can be expected.

MARILLA: Mr. Spencer, there's been a strange mistake somewhere. We sent word to Mrs. Spencer for you to bring us a boy.

MR. SPENCER: My sincere apologies. I was expressly told, "Miss Cuthbert and her brother wish to adopt a *girl*." (*To Audience*) Puzzles me how Mabel could have gotten it switched like that!

MARILLA: The asylum will take her back, won't they?

MR. SPENCER: (*Eager*) Frankly, I don't think that will be necessary. Mrs. Blewitt was telling the wife how much she wanted a girl.

MRS. BLEWITT: (*Crosses in*) Got a heap of squalling young'uns and can't hardly keep any help.

MR. SPENCER: (*Persuavive*) I think Anne will be the very girl for her. Now, I call it providential. Yes, positively providential!

MARILLA: I suppose. . . . (*To Audience*) Nobody deserves Mrs. Blewitt.

MR. SPENCER: (*Crosses to bench, getting out document and pen*) Yes, indeed! I call it a stroke of good fortune that Mrs. Blewitt happened by. We can settle the whole matter straight away! (*Sits*)

MRS. BLEWITT: (*Snarls*) Had to fire three servant girls last month. And this week two more up and quit on me!

MR. SPENCER: I think Anne here will be just the thing for you, Mrs. Blewitt!

MRS. BLEWITT: Come here, girl! (*ANNE takes a few steps; BLEWITT yanks HER over*) Have you got a name?

ANNE: (*Falters*) Anne. . . Shirley. . . .

MRS. BLEWITT: Humph! Don't appear as if there's much to you. (*Holding out an arm*) But you're wiry. (*To Audience*) Sometimes the wiry ones are best. (*Turns*) If I take you in, you'll have to be a good girl.

ANNE: (*A whisper*) Yes, Ma'am.

MRS. BLEWITT: Good and smart--and respectful too! I expect you to earn your keep, make no bones about that.

MR. SPENCER: (*Presents paper for Marilla to sign*) Then it's settled?

MRS. BLEWITT: Yes, I s'pose I might's well take her off your hands, Miz Cuthbert. The baby's awful fractious and I'm clean wore out. If you like, I can fetch her home now. Get your things, girl. (*Going for suitcase, ANNE eyes Marilla with quiet desperation.*)

MARILLA: (*About to sign*) Well, I–I don't know. . . .

MRS. BLEWITT: What's that!

MARILLA: (*Returns pen*) I didn't say Mathew and I had absolutely decided—

MRS. BLEWITT: But Mr. Spencer said—

MARILLA: In fact, Mathew is of a mind to keep her. (*Delighted, ANNE noisily drops bag*) I simply wanted to know how the error occurred. I'd best talk it over with Mathew—

MRS. BLEWITT: You mean I come all this way for no good reason?

MARILLA: (*Crosses*) Should we choose not to keep her, we'll bring the child over tomorrow night. Will that suit you, Mrs. Blewitt?

MRS. BLEWITT: (*Face to face*) S'pose it'll have to, *Miz* Cuthbert! (*Stomps off muttering*) Wasted a whole mornin'. . .

MR. SPENCER: (*Flustered*) Evening, Miss Cuthbert. Sorry about the mixup. (*Chasing after*) Sorry, Mrs. Blewitt. Guess I misunderstood—again.

ANNE: Oh Miss Cuthbert—will you really let me stay at Green Gables?

MARILLA: Isn't decided yet. We may let Mrs. Blewitt take you after all. She certainly needs you more.

ANNE: I'd rather go back to the orphanage than live with Mrs. Blewitt. She looks exactly like—like a weasel!

MARILLA: You should be ashamed! Hold your tongue and behave yourself.

ANNE: I'll do anything you want—if only you'll keep me.

MARILLA: Put your suitcase away. (*ANNE crosses*) Remember to wipe your feet. And don't let the flies in.

(ANNE departs with suitcase. MATHEW enters Up Right with milk pail.)

MATHEW: *(Hopeful)* Saw Mr. Spencer drive off.

MARILLA: Yes.

MATHEW: What's that Mrs. Blewitt doing hereabouts?

MARILLA: Mrs. Blewitt wanted to take Anne.

MATHEW: I wouldn't give a mangy dog to that Blewitt woman.

MARILLA: It's that or keeping the child ourselves. Seems sort of a duty.

MATHEW: *(Beams, encouraged)* Well now--

MARILLA: Since you're so set on it--I suppose I'm willing--to give it a try--for a few months anyway. As kind of --an experiment.

MATHEW: *(Delighted)* Experiment! Yes! Whatever you say, Marilla.

MARILLA: I might make a terrible mess of things. But if you want, the girl can stay. *On a temporary basis!*

MATHEW: I reckoned you'd come to see it in that light! Marilla, she's such a bright little thing.

MARILLA: More to the point if she was a useful little thing. But I'll see to it she's trained up proper. *(SHE crosses to kitchen.)*

MATHEW: *(Follows)* Fine. That's fine, Marilla.

MARILLA: And don't go interfering with my methods. You let me manage her.

MATHEW: Fine, Marilla. You can do the bringing up.

MARILLA: I guess an old maid knows more than an old bachelor.

MATHEW: Well now, the child will need schooling. She's a smart one. *(Pours milk into crock on counter)*

MARILLA: I'll enroll her in Sunday School right off. In

fall, Anne can start to Avonlea school--*if* she stays.

MATHEW: Well now--she'll need clothes, pretty dresses and such. (*Takes crock to pantry*)

MARILLA: I don't believe in pampering vanity. I'll make simple, serviceable dresses.

MATHEW: (*Returns*) There, there, Marilla. Have it your own way. Just be good and kind as you can--without spoiling her, of course.

MARILLA: When I fail, it'll be time enough for you to put your oar in.

MATHEW: You going to tell her tonight?

MARILLA: Heavens, no--she wouldn't sleep a wink. (*MATHEW exits to yard with pail*) Marilla Cuthbert, you've put your hand to the plow and there's no looking back! And to think Mathew should be behind it all!

(*LIGHTS UP in bedroom: In nightgown, ANNE sits at window.*)

ANNE: Goodnight, bubbling brook--apple blossoms. I always say goodnight to things I love. But it's no use loving Green Gables if you have to be torn away.

MARILLA: (*Crosses*) It's high time you said your prayers and got to bed.

ANNE: Oh, I never say prayers.

MARILLA: That's a very shameful girl!

ANNE: Mrs. Thomas said God made my hair red on purpose--so I've never cared about him since.

MARILLA: Under my roof, you will kneel down and say your prayers!

ANNE: Why can't you go into a great field--look up into the blue sky--and just feel a prayer?

MARILLA: Ask humbly for what you want and thank God for your blessings!

ANNE: (*Kneels*) Gracious heavenly Father, I thank thee for White Way of Delight, and Lake of Shining Waters. And please let me stay at Green Gables.   And please, please let me be good-looking when I grow up. I remain: Yours respectfully, Anne Shirley. Well?

MARILLA: (*Smiles*) Maybe an amen would do better. (*Crosses out*)

ANNE: (*Stops her*) Oh, Miss Cuthbert, please tell me if you're going to send me away. I can't bear not knowing.

MARILLA: (*Relents*) Well. . . Mathew and I have decided to keep you--for the time being. But only if you manage to behave.

ANNE: I'll try but it will be uphill work. Mrs. Thomas said I was desperately wicked! Can I call you Aunt Marilla?

MARILLA: Plain Marilla will do.

ANNE: It would make me feel as if I really belonged to you.

MARILLA: I am not your aunt.

ANNE: We could imagine.

MARILLA: I prefer to see things just as they are.

ANNE: Oh Miss Cuthbert--I mean--Marilla--*how much you miss*!

MARILLA: You'll learn to control that imagination. Now go to sleep and give your tongue a rest!   (*In kitchen*) About time somebody adopted that child. She's next door to a perfect heathen! Well, we've decided on the experiment and goodness knows what will come of it. (*Exits*)

(*LIGHTS UP DOWN RIGHT: RACHEL crosses to bench.*)

RACHEL: Of all things that are or ever will be--an old maid and bachelor taking in a--Total Stranger! She's been there for weeks and I've yet to lay eyes on the creature! Account of my laryngitis. (*Sits*)

MARILLA: (*Crosses to bench with sewing*) Evening, Rachel.

RACHEL: I heard about the mistake. Couldn't you send her back?

MARILLA: I suppose. But Mathew took a fancy to her right off. And I--kind of like her myself. Though she has her faults, Lord knows.

RACHEL: No telling how a child like that will turn out. But I don't want to discourage you, Marilla.

MARILLA: I've decided to give it a fair try--an experiment, you might say.

RACHEL: (*To Audience*) Pure insanity is what I say.

MARILLA: Place is more cheerful already--never know what she'll say next!

ANNE: (*Gallops on*) I found a spring in the woods--near the maple trees. Maples are such sociable trees, always rustling and whispering to you. (*Shows*) And I found ferns and June bells--

MARILLA: Settle down and stop jabbering. Anne, this is Mrs. Lynde. (*ANNE curtsies*)

RACHEL: (*Circles*) Well, they didn't pick you out for your looks, that's sure and certain! (*Peers through glasses*) She's terrible skinny and homely, Marilla. Come here, child-- and let me have a look at you. (*Pulls Anne closer*) Lawful heart, did anyone ever see such freckles? And hair as red as carrots!

ANNE: I hate you! I hate you! I hate you! How dare you call me skinny and ugly. How dare you say I'm freckled and red-headed. You are a rude, impolite woman! (*Hurls flowers at Rachel*)

MARILLA: (*Rising in horror*) Anne!

ANNE: (*Raging*) How would you like to be told you're dull and clumsy and probably don't have a spark of imagination. I don't care if I do hurt your feelings. You hurt mine worse than ever and I'll never forgive you. (*Stamping feet wildly*) Never! Never!

RACHEL: Did anybody ever see such a fit of temper!

MARILLA: (*Furious*) Anne, go to your room and stay there till I come!

ANNE: Ohhhh! (*Races in, flings herself on bed*)

RACHEL: I don't envy your job bringing that thing up, Marilla.

MARILLA: You shouldn't have spoken so blunt about her looks, Rachel.

RACHEL: Marilla Cuthbert--upholding such a frightful display of temper!

MARILLA: I'm not trying to excuse her. She's been very naughty and needs a good. . . talking-to. (*Gathers flowers*)

RACHEL: I've brought up ten and buried two. If you want my advice--which I'm sure you don't--you'll do that talking with a sturdy switch!

MARILLA: Exceptions must be made. Anne's never been taught what's right.

RACHEL: My, yes! The tender feelings of orphans-- brought in from Lord knows where--must be considered above all else!

MARILLA: You *were* too hard on her, Rachel.

RACHEL: (*Exiting*) You'll have trouble with that young one. Seems her temper matches her hair! (*To Audience*) Wait till Bertha MacPherson hears this!

MARILLA: (*Stomps to bedroom*) Anne!   Get up this minute and listen to me. *(Anne rises)* I am ashamed. You've no right to fly into such a fury.

ANNE: She had no right to call me ugly and red-headed.

MARILLA: You say it yourself often enough.

ANNE: That's different. (*Sits on bed*)

MARILLA: I don't say Mrs. Lynde is right. But that is no excuse. Rachel is my oldest friend. And you'll tell her you're sorry.

ANNE: Lock me up in a dark, damp dungeon with snakes and toads--feed me bread and water--but I can never ask Mrs. Lynde to forgive me.

MARILLA: Dungeons are rather scarce in Avonlea. But you will stay in that room till you're ready to apologize. And that's final!

ANNE: I can't even imagine I'm sorry.

MARILLA: Perhaps your imagination will improve by morning. (*In kitchen*) She'll get her meals regular. I don't believe in starving people into good behavior. (*FADE*)

(*LIGHTS UP LEFT: Carrying pitchfork, MATHEW crosses to window.*)

MATHEW: (*Kneels, whispering*) Anne. . . Anne. . . are you making it, Anne?

ANNE: (*Sits at window*) I feel so ashamed. . . .

MATHEW: Rachel Lynde is a meddlesome old gossip. Serves her right.

ANNE: When I woke this morning I wasn't angry anymore.

MATHEW: Well now, Anne. . . just do it right off and have it over with.

ANNE: (*Horrified*) You mean *apologize* to Mrs. Lynde?

MATHEW: Yes--apologize--that's the very word I was trying to get at.

ANNE: I could never face Mrs. Lynde. I'd rather stay shut up forever.

MATHEW: It'll have to be done sooner or later, Anne. Marilla's a dreadful determined woman.

ANNE: It's too humiliating. I'd rather go to Mrs. Blewitt's--

MATHEW: That slave driver--she'd work you to death.

ANNE: I'm a failure. Just send me back to the orphanage.

MATHEW: No--don't say that.

ANNE: Do you really want me to stay?

MATHEW: The kitchen's a fearful lonesome place. . . without you, Anne.

ANNE: Oh, Mathew--I'd do anything for your sake.

MATHEW: Just go smooth it over, so to speak. (*Anne rises*) That's a good girl.

ANNE: (*Decisive*) I shall tell Marilla that I have at last repented.

MATHEW: (*Concerned*) But don't tell her I said anything!

ANNE: I swear.

MATHEW: She might think I was putting my oar in when I promised not to.

ANNE: Wild horses couldn't drag it from me. (*Relieved, Mathew exits*) How can wild horses do that anyway? (*Crosses*) Marilla!

MARILLA: (*Enters kitchen*) Yes?

ANNE: I'm sorry I lost my temper and I'm willing to tell Mrs. Lynde.

MARILLA: (*To Audience*) I knew she'd come round if I

waited long enough. Very well, Miss Shirley. We'll go this minute before you change your mind. (*Doffs apron, crosses with ANNE*)

(*LIGHTS DOWN RIGHT: RACHEL sits on bench with vegetable basket.*)

MARILLA: Just don't say anything too *startling*! Good day, Rachel. (*ANNE turns suddenly, dramatically flinging herself at Rachel's feet--much to Rachel's amazement.*)

ANNE: (*From floor*) Oh Mrs. Lynde--never could I express all my sorrow--even if I used up a whole dictionary! I've disgraced the dear friends who let me stay at Green Gables even though I'm not a boy. I deserve to be cast out by respectable people--forever and ever and ever. (*Crumples*)

MARILLA: (*To Audience*) She's certainly enjoying herself enough!

RACHEL: Well, maybe what I said was harsh--

ANNE: Every word was true. My hair is red and I'm freckled and ugly. But what I said was true also! (*More shock; quick glance to Marilla*) Although I shouldn't have said it! Oh Mrs. Lynde, please forgive me or you will inflict lifelong grief on a poor orphan girl. (*To Marilla, offhand*) Was that too startling?

RACHEL: There, there. Get up, child. Of course, I forgive you. I'm such an outspoken person. So you mustn't mind me, Anne.

MARILLA: (*Wry*) Spelled with an E.

RACHEL: (*Stands*) Anne, I once knew a girl with hair as red as yours. But when she grew up, it darkened to a handsome auburn.

ANNE: (*Whirls Left*) Oh Mrs. Lynde, you have given me

a ray of hope.

RACHEL: Marilla, she may turn out all right--providing you keep her a while.

ANNE: Mrs. Lynde, do you suppose I'll find a bosom friend in Avonlea?

RACHEL: (*Aghast*) A *bosom* what!

ANNE: A bosom friend. You know--a kindred spirit--like Mathew.

MARILLA: (*To Audience*) They're both peculiar if that's what she means.

ANNE: Someone my own age. Someone I can confide in --with all my soul.

RACHEL: There's Diana Barry. Though her mother's awful particular.

MARILLA: I told Mrs. Barry I'd send you after an apron pattern. So you'll be meeting Diana after all.

ANNE: Oh Marilla, how splendid!

MARILLA: (*Exiting*) Don't let Mrs. Barry hear about your imaginary friends! She might think you're soft in the head.

RACHEL: (*Follows*) About time that child had a live playmate. (*DIANA appears Up Left with doting MOTHER to send her off.*)

ANNE: (*Crosses Center*) I hope Diana's pretty with lovely dark hair. Not red haired and homely. Such an elegant name: Diana! But I'm trembling with fear. What if Diana doesn't like me? That would be the most *tragical disappointment* of my life.

MARILLA: (*Appears Right*) And don't use all those long words!

DIANA: (*Crosses, offering book*) I heard you liked books. This one's thrilling: The heroine has five lovers.

ANNE: I'm be thankful with just one lover, wouldn't you?

DIANA: The heroine has terrible troubles and faints all the

time.

ANNE: I wish I could faint, don't you Diana? It's so romantic.

DIANA: Mother says I keep my nose buried in books. She thinks I'd get some fresh air--if I had a pal.

ANNE: We can walk in the woods--

DIANA: Collect shells on the seashore.

ANNE: Diana, could you possibly like me--enough to be my bosom friend?

DIANA: (*Happy*) I'm glad you've come to Green Gables. There are no girls close by--except my sister Minnie Mae--and she's just a baby.

ANNE: (*Suddenly seizes her hand*) Swear you will be my friend for ever and ever--

DIANA: Isn't swearing dreadfully wicked? Mrs. Lynde says:

RACHEL: (*Momentarily pops on somewhere*) Swearing is the first step on the road to the devil's front door!

ANNE: It just means promising solemnly.

DIANA: Well, I can do that.

ANNE: First we join hands over running water-- (*They look about*) Pretend this path is running water! Then I say, "I, Anne Shirley, solemnly swear to be faithful to my bosom friend, Diana Barry, as long as the sun and moon endureth." Now you.

DIANA: I, Diana Barry, solemnly swear to be faithful to my bosom friend, Anne Shirley--

ANNE: Spelled with an E.

DIANA: "As long as the sun and moon endureth." (*Both laugh*) You're an odd girl, Anne. But I think I like you.

ANNE: Marilla said not to talk you to death.

DIANA: I'm still breathing, thank you.

MRS. BARRY: (*Offstage*) Diana!

DIANA: (*Runs off, turns*) The Sunday school's having a picnic. You're invited too! Mrs. Lynde is making ice cream! (*Exits*)

ANNE: How magnificent! (*To Audience*) Was that a long word? (*FADE*)

(*LIGHTS UP in kitchen: As ANNE returns home, MATHEW reads paper in rocker. MARILLA sets down a pitifully plain dress, calls:*)

MARILLA: Anne! Anne Shirley, you come in--right this minute!

ANNE: (*Runs in*) Marilla! Marilla! Can I go to the picnic? Please? I've never even tasted ice cream.

MARILLA: I'd like to know why you can't obey me?

ANNE: Some people are naturally good--I guess I'm one of the others!

MARILLA: You were supposed to be home hours ago!

ANNE: Marilla, it's harder to be good when you have red hair. Besides, Diana and I had so much to talk about--we're bosom friends.

MARILLA: If you weren't so feather-brained, you'd keep track of the time.

ANNE: I'm sorry, Marilla. I won't be late again. One good thing about me: I never make the same mistake twice!

MARILLA: What good is that? You keep making new ones.

ANNE: Oh Marilla, I'll absolutely perish if I don't go to the picnic.

MARILLA: I may be strict and set in my ways, but I don't approve of girls gadding about all over creation--

ANNE: Please, Marilla. Can I go? Please. (*Mathew loudly clears his throat.*)

MARILLA: (*Looks his way*) *However*, . . since it's a Sunday school outing--

ANNE: Oh thank you, Marilla. (*Abruptly kisses her*)

MARILLA: (*Embarrassed*) Never mind your kissing nonsense. I'd sooner see you doing exactly as you're told.

ANNE: Ice cream! I can't even imagine what it tastes like!

MARILLA: Here's a new calico for the picnic. (*Sees Anne's disappointment*) Aren't you grateful?

ANNE: I'm very grateful, Marilla. But puffed sleves are so stylish.

MARILLA: I haven't material to waste on puffed sleeves. They look ridiculous. I much prefer plain, sensible ones.

ANNE: I'd rather look ridiculous like everyone else--than plain and sensible all by myself!

MARILLA: Trust you for that. Now, put your dress away neat.

MATHEW: I heard you liked chocolates. So I brought some from town. (*Presents small paper bag. Thrilled, ANNE kisses his cheek, then crosses to her bedroom. Laying down the dress, SHE sits in the DIM LIGHT, savoring chocolates.*)

MARILLA: You should have bought peppermints. They're wholesomer.

MATHEW: Seems like she's always been here.

MARILLA: Today she let the pie burn up in the oven. Still, I can't picture the place without her--muddleheaded though she is. (*Mathew grins slyly*) Now don't be looking like "I told you so."

MATHEW: Now, Marilla--

MARILLA : I admit I'm getting fond of her but as far as

I'm concerned, she's still on trial. (*Exits to hall*)

MATHEW: (*Stands*) I didn't say a word. (*FADE. HE takes cap, exits to yard.*)

(*LIGHTS UP in bedroom: ANNE sits, still enjoying candy.*)

ANNE: If anything keeps me from that picnic, it will be my lifelong sorrow. Mrs. Lynde says:

RACHEL: (*Pops on somewhere else*) Blessed are they who expect nothing, for they shall not be disappointed.

ANNE: But I think expecting nothing is far worse.

MARILLA: (*Enters*) Anne, did you see my amethyst brooch? I stuck the brooch in my pin cushion when I came home from church.

ANNE: I passed by your door so I went in to look. Do you suppose amethysts are the souls of good violets?

MARILLA: Did you touch my brooch?

ANNE: Y-e-e-s. I pinned it on--to see how it would look.

MARILLA: You had no business meddling in my room. Where did you put it?

ANNE: Back on your dresser. On the pincushion--or the china tray.

MARILLA: It's not on the dresser. Tell the truth, did you take my brooch?

ANNE: (*Stands*) I am telling the truth. Even if I'm led to the block for it. Though I'm not exactly sure what a block is.

MARILLA: You'll stay here until you confess. Make up your mind to that!

ANNE: But the picnic is today! Let me out for the picnic and I'll stay as long as you like afterward.

MARILLA: Until you confess, there'll be no picnic!

(*Crosses to kitchen.   Making her decision, ANNE marches to closet with dress.*)

MATHEW: (*Enters back door*) What's wrong, Marilla?

MARILLA: Mother's amethyst brooch is gone.   Anne probably lost it and is afraid to own up.

MATHEW: Maybe it fell behind the dresser.

MARILLA: I searched every crack and cranny. Mathew, I put up with her fits of temper, but I won't stand for dishonesty!

MATHEW: Well now. . . maybe it fell into a drawer.

MARILLA: I emptied the drawers.

MATHEW: Well now, maybe--

MARILLA: Mathew, the child not only took the brooch but lied.   That's the pure ugly truth and we may as well face it.

MATHEW: (*Worried*) Well now. . . what are you going to do?

MARILLA: She'll stay in that room till she confesses.   In any case, the girl will be severely punished.

MATHEW: Well now, I've nothing to do with that, Marilla.   (*Sits in rocker*) You warned me not to put my oar in.

MARILLA: Her dishonesty hurts me far more than losing Mother's brooch.

ANNE: (*Strides on wearing picnic dress*) Marilla, I'm ready to confess.

MARILLA: Let me hear what you have to say, child.

ANNE: (*Performs, facing front*) I took the brooch--yearning to play Lady Cordelia with a real amethyst.   At the bridge over Shining Waters--suddenly it slipped through my fingers--like so.   And sailed down--down--down--all purple and sparkly--sinking forever.   (*Turns*) That's the best I can do at confessing, Marilla.

MARILLA: Anne, you are the wickedest girl I ever heard of!

ANNE: (*Matter of fact*) Yes, I suppose so. And it's your duty to punish me. So please get it over with. Because I'd like to enjoy the picnic with nothing on my mind!

MARILLA: PICNIC INDEED! You'll go to no picnic today!

ANNE: (*Wild*) But you promised!   That is why I confessed. Punish me any way you like. But please--please let me go. This may be my only chance to taste ice cream!

MARILLA: NO!   AND THAT'S FINAL.   NOT ANOTHER WORD.

ANNE: (*Shrieks, running to bedroom*) OHHHHH!

MARILLA: Lord, that child is crazy or worse. I'm afraid Rachel was right.

MATHEW: Well now. . . I admit she did wrong. . . but Anne was so set on that picnic.

MARILLA: Mathew Cuthbert, I'm amazed at you. The girl doesn't even realize how wicked she's been. That's what troubles me most.

MATHEW: Well now, she's such a young thing. Allowances should be made.

MARILLA: Count on you to make excuses. She goes right back to the asylum! I won't tolerate sinfulness in my home.

MATHEW: Marilla, you know Anne's never had any real bringing up.

MARILLA: The asylum can attend to that, thank you. Need to mend my black lace shawl. (*Takes shawl off hook*)

MATHEW: Don't bother with dinner. (*Rising, clutches heart in pain*)

MARILLA: Mathew? Something wrong?

MATHEW: No--nothing--just not hungry. (*Exits back door, still in pain; troubled, Marilla watches*)

MARILLA: Dear life and heart! My brooch! I thought it was at the bottom of Barry's Pond! I remember--after church--I laid my shawl on the dresser. Must be the brooch got caught somehow-- (*MARILLA strides into bedroom. ANNE sits, staring out of window.*)

ANNE: No dinner please, my heart is broken. Besides, pork and greens are so unpoetical when one is in affliction.

MARILLA: Anne Shirley! I found my brooch snagged to this shawl. What was that rigamarole you just recited?

ANNE: You said I'd stay till I confessed. Seems my effort was wasted.

MARILLA: Anne, you do beat all. But I drove you to confess. So if you'll forgive me, we'll start square again. Time to get ready for the picnic.

ANNE: Oh, Marilla, I won't be too late?

MARILLA: They're not half gathered yet. Wash your face, comb your hair and I'll do up your basket. (*Crosses to kitchen*)

ANNE: Five minutes ago I was wishing I'd never been born. And now I wouldn't trade places with an angel! (*Exits*)

MARILLA: That child is hard to fathom. Never saw anything in my life to equal her! (*Beams*) Maybe school can settle her down. (*Alarm*) But goodness knows the trouble she might stir up there! (*FADE*)

(*LIGHTS UP DOWNSTAGE: ANNE enters Up Right, crosses Center.*)

ANNE: (*In picnic dress*) The picnic this afternoon was scrumptious. That's a word I learned today. Prissy Andrews fell overboard and nearly drowned--except Mr. Phillips caught her by the sash. So romantic to nearly drown. As for ice cream--words fail me. But I assure you: It was an epoch in my life! (*Quick BLACKOUT*)

MARILLA: (*Calls, during blackout*) Be a good girl. Don't talk too much. Don't get into fights. And don't sass the teacher.

ANNE: (*Offstage*) Yes, Marilla.

(*LIGHTS UP DOWNSTAGE: JOSIE and GILBERT enter, setting stools Down Center. Fancy ribbons and curls adorn Josie.*)

GILBERT: (*Interested*) Josie, who's this Miss Shirley person anyway?

JOSIE: Just an orphan girl from the asylum. Isn't that red hair something awful!

GILBERT: Maybe. (*Laughs, teasing*) Then again--maybe not!

JOSIE: (*Stamping her foot, whines*) Gilbert!

(*Noisy STUDENTS enter with small stools. MOODY and CHARLEY place blackboard Down Left. Students sit lined up facing front. JOSIE primps with mirror. CHARLIE, a likeable clown, and MOODY, overly serious, draws on slates. RUBY, given to hysterics, works on sums. Pointer in hand, Gilbert shows off at the blackboard.*)

GILBERT: Class, attention please. Oh, Miss Shirley--

ANNE: (*Stands, Right*) He winked at me!

DIANA: (*Grins*) Gilbert's a terrible tease. But isn't he

good-looking?

    ANNE: Hardly good manners to wink at a strange girl!

    DIANA: He's smart, too. Always head of the class.

    ANNE: Mrs. Hammond barely ever let me go to school--account of the twins. So I'm way behind. And Mr. Phillips called me a dunce!

    DIANA: Don't mind Phillips--he doesn't know anything-- (*Offstage, MR. PHILLIPS rings bell. GILBERT dashes to seat.*)

    ANNE: (*Points*) And Josie--

    DIANA: (*Whispers*) Was born mean. Just ignore her. (*THEY sit. As MR. PHILLIPS enters, STUDENTS sit, frozen in fear. Left to Right, CHARLIE, MOODY, RUBY, GILBERT, JOSIE, DIANE, ANNE.*)

    MR. PHILLIPS: Recess is over. Slates out: Time to check your sums. (*Crosses behind stools. STUDENTS hold up their slates for his approval*)

    CHARLIE: Sorry, Mr. Phillips. (*MR. PHILLIPS swats him with pointer*)

    MR. PHILLIPS: Very good, Ruby. (*Marking huge "X"*) All wrong, Moody.

    MOODY: (*Hopeful smile vanishes*) I tried my best, Mr. Phillips.

    MR. PHILLIPS: (*Noisily striking slate*) Not good enough, Moody. (*Continues down row, nodding*) And now our new pupil, Miss Shirley. Well, I can see they did not emphasize arithmetic at your former school. (*Strikes slate; JOSIE snickers*)

    RUBY: You said we'd finish our spelling bee after recess, Mr. Phillips.

    MR. PHILLIPS: Oh yes. Slates down. Close your spelling books. Who's still up? (*GILBERT, JOSIE, ANNE,*

MOODY, RUBY rise; RUBY shoves MOODY down.   Opens book) Ruby's first: "Category."

RUBY: I know it--I know it-- "Category": C A T A G O R Y.

MR. PHILLIPS: *(Pushes her down with pointer)* Quite wrong.

MOODY: I never get the easy ones.

MR. PHILLIPS: *(Crosses Right)* Josie Pye: "Omitted."

JOSIE: O M M-- *(Peeks into book, held open at her side)* I T E D.

MR. PHILLIPS: Very good, Josie.

ANNE: I thought it was two T's and one M.

MR. PHILLIPS: *(Checks, annoyed)* Hmmm. So it is! Er--uh--I--I misunderstood! *(JOSIE angrily sits)* Gilbert: "Knowledge."

JOSIE: *(Shows book)* Psst, Gilbert.

GILBERT: *(Ignores Josie)* "Knowledge." K N O W L E D G E.

MR. PHILLIPS: Miss Shirley: "Strength."

ANNE: *(Worried)* "Strength." S T R E N. . . T H!

MR. PHILLIPS: *(Pushes her down with pointer)* Miss Shirley, your spelling isn't quite so perfect as you think! Very good, Gilbert.

DIANA: Don't worry, Anne. Gilbert always wins.

MOODY: Why didn't I get that word?

MR. PHILLIPS: Time for your reading books.

PRISSY'S VOICE: *(Offstage)* Oh, Mr. Phillips--

MR. PHILLIPS: I'll be in the cloak room helping one of our--older students. *(Beams)* Coming, Prissy. *(Exits. Now chaos reigns. CHARLIE leaps up, crumples paper into ball.)*

CHARLIE: Here's my famous speed ball. *(Plays catch with GILBERT)*

DIANA: (*To Anne*) Mr. Phillips is dead gone on Prissy. She's sixteen and studying for her entrance exams to Queen's Academy.

CHARLIE: (*Shows slate with comic picture*) Gilbert–who's this?

GILBERT: Romeo Phillips.

CHARLIE: (*Leaping onto stool*) Romeo, Romeo. Wherefore art thou, Romeo?

GILBERT: (*Kneels*) In the cloak room! With Prissy Andrews! (*Loud laughter. MR. PHILLIPS returns. STUDENTS sit, frozen.*)

MR. PHILLIPS: Class! Quiet! Or you'll stay after school! (*Exits quickly. Chaos again.*)

MOODY: Anyone want the rest of my lunch?

GILBERT: (*Offers*) Trade you for an apple.

RUBY: (*Jumps up screaming*) Somebody put a tack on my seat! I might have been fatally injured!

MR. PHILLIPS: (*Enters*) Who's going to stay after school today? Who's going to get his bottom switched with rawhide? (*Fearful silence*)

PRISSY'S VOICE: Oh, Mr. Phillips–

MR. PHILLIPS: (*Beams*) Coming, Prissy. (*Another hasty exit*)

RUBY: (*Rubbing bottom*) Was that you, Charlie?

CHARLIE: (*Grins*) Would I do a thing like that? (*Class nods "yes"*)

GILBERT: Hey, Ruby Red Lips, want some candy?

CHARLIE: (*Snatches his slate*) Moody! Let's dance. (*Whirls him around– Moody reaching for slate*)

MOODY: Charlie–I'm studying. (*Reclaims slate*)

GILBERT: (*Stands*) Ohhh Miss Shirley– (*ANNE ignores him*)

JOSIE: Gilbert, did you see all the freckles on that poor orphan girl? (*GILBERT crosses behind ANNE's stood. DIANA slips a note to ANNE.*)

GILBERT: (*Seizes*) Is that for me? Oh thank you, Diana. (*Scoots Right*)

ANNE: (*Retrieves*) For your information, the note is addressed to me!

GILBERT: (*Mimicks*) Miss Shirley, how do you spell carrots? (*Yanks on her braids*) "Carrots": C A R R--

ANNE: How dare you! You mean hateful boy! (*ANNE shatters her slate over GILBERT's head. Slate pieces fly. General commotion. STUDENTS run to his rescue.*)

RUBY: (*Screams*) OHHH. Anne murdered Gilbert!

JOSIE: Are you bleeding, Gilbert? (*Seeing MR. PHILLIPS enter, STUDENTS flee to seats. ANNE holds remains of slate.*)

MR. PHILLIPS: Anne Shirley, what is the meaning of this?

GILBERT: (*Nursing head*) It was my fault, Mr. Phillips. I teased her.

MR. PHILLIPS: What a display of temper and vindictive spirit! Anne Shirley, come to the blackboard. (*Crosses; writes:*) "Ann Shirley has a bad temper." Copy that sentence. (*JOSIE giggles; ANNE angrily adds large "E" before copying.*)

JOSIE: That she-devil almost killed you, Gilbert!

MR. PHILLIPS: Tomorrow you will write this sentence one hundred times. That should teach you to control your temper! (*Rings bell*) Class dismissed. (*Exits. STUDENTS flee with stools and blackboard.*)

CHARLIE: That girl is dangerous!

GILBERT: I'm awfully sorry I made fun of your hair, Anne. Honest I am. Don't be mad for keeps.

ANNE: I shall never speak to you again as long as I draw breath.

GILBERT: I was just having some fun. Here--would you like a candy heart? (*ANNE hurls it away*) Then be that way. I said I was sorry! (*In a fury, HE exits with books, stool*)

DIANA: (*With stool*) Don't mind Gilbert. He torments all us girls--calls me Crow-hair.   And I've never heard him apologize before.

ANNE: My soul has turned to iron. I shall never forgive Mr. Blythe. Not till the end of time. Not for eons.

DIANA: *Eons*? What's an eon?

ANNE: I'm not sure--I read it in a book once. (*GIRLS exit*)

(*LIGHTS UP in kitchen: MARILLA sets table.*)

MATHEW: (*Enters with firewood*) Tea ready?

MARILLA: No--tea is not ready. Because of your Miss Anne! Rather than come straight home and do her chores-- she's off gallivanting.

MATHEW: Well now. . . you're judging a mite hasty.

MARILLA: She needs to be pulled up short and sudden, that's what.

MATHEW: Must be some reason she's gone.

MARILLA: The minute she grows out of one quirk--she takes up another. (*ANNE enters from closet, her hair covered by a huge kerchief. SHE sits in despair, head resting on vanity.*)

MATHEW: Maybe it can all be explained. Anne's a great one for explaining.

MARILLA: Trust you to take her part. But I'm bringing her up--not you! I'll call when tea's ready. (*MATHEW takes wood to pantry. Looking into mirror, ANNE groans.*)

ANNE: OHHHHHH. (*Throws herself on bed*)

MARILLA: (*Crosses to bedroom*) Gracious sakes! What are you doing here! Are you sick!

ANNE: Please, Marilla. Go away and don't look at me. This has been the worst day of my entire life.

MARILLA: Do I dare ask what you did at school today?

ANNE: I broke my slate over Gilbert Blythe's head.

MARILLA: And why was that?

ANNE: He called me Carrots. And Mr. Phillips insulted me too. My life is over. I'll never leave this room. Except to go back to the orphanage. Please Marilla, go away.

MARILLA: Anne Shirley! Whatever is the matter with you? Get right up this minute and tell me. This minute!

ANNE: (*Rises*) I'm the unhappiest girl on Prince Edward Island. (*Takes off kerchief, wails*) Look at my hair, Marilla!

MARILLA: (*Sheepish laugh*) Why Anne Shirley! Your hair is green!

ANNE: (*Bawls*) I thought red hair was awful. But green hair is ten times worse.

MARILLA: I knew things were going too smooth. What happened to your hair?

ANNE: I dyed it.

MARILLA: Dyed your hair! Do you know how sinful that is?

ANNE: I thought getting rid of red hair would be worth the risk.

MARILLA: (*Chortles in spite of herself*) Well, I would have dyed it a decent color at least.

ANNE: I didn't pick green! He said I'd have beautiful raven tresses.

MARILLA: Who did?

ANNE: The peddler who drove by. He said my "rich lustrous black" would never wash off.

MARILLA: Perhaps you've learned how vanity can lead you astray.

ANNE: (*Blubbers louder*) He told the truth about one thing: I scrubbed and scrubbed and it won't wash off!

MARILLA: You can't go around looking like that.

ANNE: I'll never return to school again. Josie Pye would laugh at me. And Gilbert—I mean—the boys would think I'm a disgrace.

MARILLA: (*Goes to kitchen*) We'll have to cut it off—there's no other way.

ANNE: All I do is get into trouble.

MARILLA: (*Calls*) You haven't been in a scrape for a week. It was overdue.

ANNE: You'll want to send me back. I failed the trial.

MARILLA: (*Returns with scissors*) You are a trial, if truth be told.

ANNE: And I did so want to please Mathew—because he wanted me.

MARILLA: (*A difficult admission*) We. . . we both want you, Anne.

ANNE: You're not going to send me back?

MARILLA: I shall have my hands full and no mistake—but you'll live right here, with us.

ANNE: I'll be Anne of Green Gables? Forever?

MARILLA: For as long as you like! (*ANNE reaches to kiss her. MARILLA pulls away, awkwardly.*) But you will return to school. (*Sets chair for haircut*) You're not so smart that Mr. Phillips can't teach you a thing or two.

ANNE: Oh Marilla, I shall devote all my energies to being good and never try to be beautiful again. (*Sits in chair*)

MARILLA: It's vain to think about your looks so much.

ANNE: How can I be vain when I'm so homely?

MARILLA: Handsome is as handsome does. (*Covers Anne's shoulders with kerchief*)

ANNE: It's nice to know tomorrow's a new day with no mistakes.

MARILLA: (*With scissors*) I'll warrant you'll make plenty.

ANNE: There must be a limit to the mistakes one person can make. When I get to the end--I'll be through forever!

MARILLA: That's a very comforting thought.

ANNE: This has turned out to be a splendid day after all. Oh Marilla, what would the year be with no September!

MARILLA: About eleven months. (*Cuts hair as LIGHTS FADE*)

(*LIGHTS UP DOWNSTAGE: RACHEL enters, putting on hat.*)

RACHEL: That Anne girl looked like a plucked chicken--till her hair finally grew back. Red as ever! In June, Mr. Phillips ups and resigns. If you want my opinion--which I'm sure you don't--only reason he got hired is because his uncle's on the school board. Canada's going to the dogs, mark my words. Well, it's plain proof: Things can't be perfect in an imperfect world. (*Sits on bench*) Marilla!

MARILLA: (*Enters with hat*) I'll be right out, Rachel. Anne, don't be dawdling! Anne! Might's well be calling the wind.

ANNE: (*Enters*) Oh Marilla, I want to be extra good today! Because it's an anniversary. Do you remember what happened this day last year?

MARILLA: No. Can't think of anything special.

ANNE: It wouldn't seem important to you but that day marked an epoch in my life: The day I came to Green Gables!

RACHEL: Marilla!

ANNE: Of course I've had my troubles. Are you sorry you kept me?

MARILLA: No, I can't say I'm sorry. (*Puts on hat*) Not *exactly* sorry.

RACHEL: Marilla!

MARILLA: It's true you're settling down a bit. (*Sets tea pot on table*) That's why I invited Diana to tea.

ANNE: How lovely. (*Hug*) Thanks, Marilla.

MARILLA: (*Pushing away*) That's enough now. Open the preserves, cut the fruitcake-- Don't know if I'm doing the right thing.

ANNE: We'll be perfect ladies! I assure you!

MARILLA: There's raspberry cordial in the pantry--offer Diana the cordial.

RACHEL: (*Crossing to door*) Marilla! We're late for Ladies' Aid!

MARILLA: (*Leaving*) And keep your wits about you, for heaven's sake.

ANNE: Marilla, I'm over thirteen! By next year I'll be grown up!

MARILLA: (*To Rachel*) I may be making a terrible mistake. (*Elegantly outfitted, DIANA appears Left with MRS. BARRY. Fussing over Diana, MRS. BARRY beams, waves goodbye. Crossing, DIANA curtsies to ladies as they pass.*)

ANNE: (*Returns with cordial tray*) I'll ask Diana if she takes sugar. She doesn't but I'll ask anyway. (*DIANA arrives --quite proper. GIRLS greet in formal fashion.*)

DIANA: Good afternoon, Anne. And how is Mr. Cuthbert?

ANNE: Very well, thank you. Please be seated. May I take your parasol?

DIANA: Thank you. I suppose Mr. Cuthbert's hauling potatoes to the dock?

ANNE: Yes, our crop is especially good this year.

DIANA: Our cucumber crop is excellent. And our turnips are doing well.

ANNE: Would you like some cordial?

DIANA: That would be ever so nice.

ANNE: Please help yourself, Diana. Excuse me. (*Exits for cake. Pouring slowly, DIANA savors cordial. SHE smiles, drinks more.*)

DIANA: Did you know Ruby Gillis has a magic pebble? It charmed all her warts away. True as you live. And Gilbert Blythe--

ANNE: (*Charges out*) Diana--I cannot allow you to speak of that person!

DIANA: (*Drinks*) Mmmm. Didn't know raspberry cordial was so pleasant.

ANNE: Have more, Diana. (*Diana obliges*)

DIANA: Much better than Mrs. Lynde's--though she brags about hers. (*Slurring words*) Strange--this doesn't taste like Lissus Mynde's. (*As ANNE chatters, DIANA guzzles--getting increasingly drunk.*)

ANNE: Marilla's trying to teach me to cook but it's uphill work. Last time I made a cake I got to daydreaming. Instead of vanilla, I flavored it with rubbing liniment. (*DIANA starts to weave in her chair.*)I was thinking of the loveliest story, Diana. You were desperately ill with small pox but I nursed you back to life.

DIANA: (*Almost falling*) Oh thank you, Anne dear.

ANNE: Then I took the small pox and died, so you

planted a rosebush at my grave and watered it with your tears.

DIANA: (*Draped across table*) Ohhhh, how saaaaad. (*Laughs abruptly*)

ANNE: You never forgot the friend of your youth who sacrificed her life-- (*Diana moans*) Diana?

DIANA: I must go right home.

ANNE: You can't go now--without your tea!

DIANA: (*Stands*) I'm awfully dizzy.

ANNE: You haven't had fruitcake. Or cherry preserves.

DIANA: (*Groans*) I feel very strange--

ANNE: (*Gets hat, parasol*) Oh Diana, perhaps you really do have small pox!

DIANA: (*Totters*) I think I'm sick.

ANNE: (*Struggles to support Diana*) I'll nurse you, Diana. I'll never forsake you. But I do wish you'd stay for tea. (*Crossing home, DIANA weaves and whirls--almost falling. ANNE staggers, trying to hold her up.*)

MRS. BARRY: (*Appears Left*) Diana Barry, whatever is the matter with you!

DIANA: (*Giggles*) I don't know. . . .

MRS. BARRY: Anne Shirley, what on earth have you done to my daughter!

DIANA: (*Laughs*) I had raspberry cordial!

MRS. BARRY: (*Sniffs*) That's not cordial! That's wine! Marilla's currant wine! Of which I have never approved!

DIANA: (*Boasts*) Three glassfuls!

MRS. BARRY: Anne Shirley, you got my daughter drunk and brought her home in this disgraceful condition. (*DIANA clamps hat on backwards, ribbon streaming down her face.*)

ANNE: I didn't mean to, Mrs. Barry. If you were a poor orphan with one bosom friend in the world--would you intoxicate her on purpose?

MRS. BARRY: I will never allow Diana to play with you again! Never!

ANNE: Then you'll cover my life with a dark cloud of woe.

MRS. BARRY: I suggest you go home and behave yourself.

DIANA: (*About to be ill*) Ohhhh nooooo. (*Runs off; MRS. BARRY follows*)

ANNE: (*Crossing home*) The next day I tried to bid Diana farewell, but Mrs. Barry slammed the door in my face. (*MARILLA enters, clears table. ANNE returns, forlorn.*)

MARILLA: You have a genius for getting into trouble. Can't you tell the difference between cordial and wine?

ANNE: (*Sits*) I never tasted it. I thought the bottle was cordial.

MARILLA: This will be a fine story with all those folks down on me for making currant wine.

ANNE: My heart is broken. Diana and I are parted forever.

MARILLA: (*Defensive*) I only make the wine for medicinal purposes.

ANNE: (*Begs*) You talk to Mrs. Barry. Please, Marilla.

MARILLA : I tried--but she wouldn't listen.

ANNE: God himself couldn't do a thing with such an obstinate person.

MARILLA: Anne! You must not talk that way!

ANNE: (*Tragic*) Now my last hope is gone. (*Crosses to bedroom*)

MARILLA: (*With bottle*) I told Julia Barry my wine was not meant to be guzzled three glasses at a time! I'd sober up Diana with a good spanking! (*Exits to pantry*)

DIANA: (*Runs to Anne's window*) Anne! Anne!

ANNE: Thank heaven, Diana. Your mother has relented!

DIANA: No! She says I'm never to speak with you again. Had to sneak out--can only stay a minute. I came to say goodbye.

ANNE: A minute isn't very long for an eternal farewell.

DIANA: I've lost my girlhood chum.

ANNE: Diana, in years to come thy memory wilt shine o'er my lonely life. Wilt thou give me a lock of thy jet black tresses?

DIANA: I don't have any *black dresses*!

ANNE: Your hair!

DIANA: Oh! (*ANNE takes scissor from pocket, cuts a wisp*)

ANNE: Fare thee well, beloved friend.

DIANA: I've got to run. (*Racing off*) Fare thee well.

ANNE: (*Waves wistfully*) Henceforth we meet as strangers. (*MARILLA enters with cordial*) Diana and I had such a lovely farewell. Thee and thou are ever so romantic. (*Sits on bed*)

MARILLA: (*Awkward*) I just remembered--the cordial was in the cellar--not the pantry.

ANNE: I've lost Diana. And my make-believe friends are gone. (*Tragic*) Marilla, I don't think I shall live very long. Perhaps when Mrs. Barry sees me lying cold and dead--(*slowly sinks back on bed.*) she will feel remorse and let Diana come to my funeral.

MARILLA: I don't think you'll die of grief. So long as you can talk.

ANNE: This lock of Diana's hair--make sure it's buried with me. (*Falls back in a heap*)

MARILLA: (*Nods with sympathy*) I promise. (*FADE*)

(LIGHTS UP DOWNSTAGE: Screaming, RUBY runs on Left with JOSIE.)

RUBY: HELP! HELP! MISS CUTHBERT! HELP! *(MARILLA hurries into yard)* Anne fell off the roof.

JOSIE: *(Frantic)* Moody and Charlie are bringing her home now!

RUBY: We were playing dare in the school yard.

JOSIE: It was just an accident, Miss Cuthbert!

RUBY: Josie said, "I dare you to climb up and walk the ridgepole!"

JOSIE: Ruby, it's not my fault!

RUBY: But I said, "Don't do it, Anne! You'll fall and kill yourself. Never mind Josie Pye!" *(MOODY and CHARLIE enter with a lifeless ANNE in their arms.)*

CHARLIE: *(To Audience, alarmed)* She stopped *talking*!

MOODY: Stopped moving--

MARILLA: *(Terrified)* Mercy me! Oh no! *(Tries to revive her)* Anne! Anne! What'll I do?

RUBY: *(Screaming)* She's killed. She's dead. OHHHH.

CHARLIE: Say something, Anne!

RUBY: Anne, dear, tell us if you're killed.

ANNE: *(Mumbles, dazed)* No, Ruby, I don't think I'm killed. But I do think I'm rendered unconscious.

RUBY: *(Stricken)* Where? Where are you unconscious, Anne?

MARILLA: *(Stands apart, shaken)* Gave me such a scare. My heart's pounding like a drum. Boys, would you carry Anne to the bedroom?

RUBY: Not right to dare anyone to do something so dangerous.

JOSIE: I walked the fence, didn't I?

RUBY: That's different.

MARILLA: (*To girls*) Mathew's out in the back pasture. Send him after Dr. Stevens. (*They run off. Struggling, BOYS set ANNE on bed with comic difficulty. Starting to lay her head at foot of bed sort of thing.*)

CHARLIE: (*Heaving ANNE onto bed*) One--two--three--

ANNE: (*Howls*) Owwww.

CHARLIE: Hope she's all right, Miss Cuthbert. (*BOYS exit*)

ANNE: (*Trying to stand, fall back in pain*) Ohhhh. I fear I've sprained my ankle.

MARILLA: For heaven's sake, what were you doing on that roof?

ANNE: I had to walk the ridge pole though I might perish in the attempt. My honor was at stake.

MARILLA: (*Unlaces shoe*) Serves you right for such tomfoolery.

ANNE: Aren't you sorry for me, Marilla?

MARILLA: It was your own doing!

ANNE: That's why you should feel sorry. If I could blame somebody else I'd feel much better.

MARILLA: Trouble is, you never stop and think!

ANNE: But Marilla, thinking it over spoils everything!

MARILLA: (*Removes shoe; Anne groans*) Dr. Stevens will have to set that ankle. You'll be off your feet for weeks.

ANNE: I'll miss school! Then Gilb--I mean--everyone will get ahead. (*Wails*) Oh, I am such an afflicted mortal!

MARILLA: One thing plain to see: The fall hasn't injured your tongue!

ANNE: (*Furious*) Marilla! If you knew all the things I'd like to say and don't--you'd give me some credit! (*MARILLA crosses to kitchen, still shaken. LIGHTS focus on two isolated figures.*)

MARILLA: Scared the living daylights out of me. Thought I'd lost her for certain. . . I couldn't bear that-- (*Stops herself*)

ANNE: (*Not comprehending*) I'm a terrible trial to Marilla. Guess that's why she had tears in her eyes.

MARILLA: (*Drawing up stiffly*) Marilla Cuthbert! It's sinful to set your heart too much on any living creature!

(*LIGHTS FADE*)

ACT TWO

RACHEL: *(Enters Down Right.)* Of all the scandalous notions! Now they've gone and hired a female teacher! If you want my opinion--which I'm sure you don't--that's a dangerous innovation. Next, folks will be wanting female ministers. Like in the United States. *(Crosses)* Whole world's turning up side down--that's sure and certain. Marilla!

MARILLA: *(Enters from pantry, pours tea)* Come in, Rachel.

RACHEL: Never heard of such goings-on at school with that new teacher.

MARILLA: Miss Stacy wears the biggest puffed sleeves in all Avonlea. Probably has to go through the door sideways.

RACHEL: Miss Stacy made my blood run cold when I saw schoolboys climb those tall tree on the hill. After a crow's nest! Whatever for?

MARILLA: Nature study! They even do skits and other such foolishness.

RACHEL: What's this about *(Horror)* *Physical Culture* exercises!

MARILLA: Supposed to promote "grace and good digestion." Fiddlesticks!

RACHEL: It all comes of having a female teacher.

MARILLA: I'm to see Miss Stacy at school today. Anne's probably in trouble again. *(Clears table)*

RACHEL: College education for women! Lord help us. *(FADE. SHE exits Right)*

(LIGHTS UP DOWNSTAGE: MISS STACY dances on from Left. GIRLS follow, swirling with comic grace. At the rear of the line, BOYS clown. MOODY places

teacher's seat Down Left.)

MISS STACY: Come, class: And one, two, three. One, two, three. Twirl around. Bend right. Bend left. Very slowly. And twirl around. Very good. Class, recess time. (*Crosses Left to seat*)

GILBERT: (*Falsetto*) Charlie, up on your toes. (*Boys do mock ballet. Down Right, DIANA and ANNE secretively trade notes.*)

ANNE: "Mother still says I'm not to talk to you. Anne, I miss you awfully. Have no one to tell my secrets to."

DIANA: "When twilight drops her curtain down and pins it with a star, remember that you have a friend, though she may travel far."

CHARLIE: I saw you put an apple by a certain person's books today.

GILBERT: Not me.

CHARLIE: (*Sing-song*) Gilbert loves Anne.

GILBERT: Her Ladyship—Miss Freckle Face? Not on your life.

RUBY: Anne, I found this apple by your chair-- (*ANNE starts to bite*) Must be from Gilbert. His Dad grows Pippins.

ANNE: (*Flings apple across to Moody*) He called me Carrots!

RUBY: That was last year! Why are you so mean to Gilbert?

ANNE: Ruby, do not mention that name in my presence.

RUBY: (*Teases*) Gil-l-l-bert?

ANNE: I shall never forget the vow I made. (*MISS STACY rings. STUDENTS gather informally, sitting on floor.*)

CHARLIE: Why do we have to write stories every week, Miss Stacy?

MISS STACY: To exercise the imagination.

CHARLIE: My imagination has arther-itis.

MISS STACY: (*Opens briefcase*) Anne, come and read the class your story.

ANNE: THE JEALOUS RIVAL. OR, IN DEATH NOT DIVIDED. By Rosamond Montmorency! (*Proud*) That's my *nom-de-plume*!

MOODY: Nom de what?

GILBERT: Means pen name, Moody.

ANNE: Once there lived two friends--Lady Cordelia, a regal brunette with midnight hair and flashing eyes--

CHARLIE: Mmmm. . . sounds good.

ANNE: And Lady Geraldine, with spun-gold hair and purple eyes--

JOSIE: I never saw anybody with purple eyes!

ANNE: (*Performs*) Handsome Lord Bertram fell in love with fair Geraldine, so down he went on bended knee--

RUBY: They don't do that nowadays! (*Shy*) I hid in the pantry when my sister got proposed to. (*Class laughs*)

ANNE: (*Extravagant gestures*) Cordelia, secretly in love with Bertram, raged with jealousy. One night, when the maidens stood by a roaring stream, Cordelia pushed Geraldine into the rapids. At once, Bertram plunged into the current. "I will save thee, my peerless one."

CHARLIE: So he rescues Geraldine and they live happily ever after!

ANNE: (*Ecstatic*) Alas, Bertram forgot he could not swim so they both drowned! (*CLASS moans*) Well, I think it's more romantic to end with a funeral than a wedding.

CHARLIE: Whatever happened to that Cordelia girl?

ANNE: She went insane with remorse and was shut up in a dark tower.

RUBY: (*Enthralled*) Oh! How perfectly lovely.

GILBERT: The one about a prisoner escaping from the dungeon--that was good too. (*ANNE turns away haughtily*) For a girl!

MOODY: (*Admiring*) Maybe you could be a writer, Anne.

ANNE: Thank you very much, *Moody*. (*He melts*)

MISS STACY: All of you need to be thinking about the future.

JOSIE: In two years I can wear my hair up.

MISS STACY: There are *important* decisions coming your way.

RUBY: I'll be a teacher--if I pass the entrance exam for Queen's. I'll teach two years and then get married.

CHARLIE: My sister's so ornery she'll never get married.

GILBERT: Charlie--you'll either wind up in politics or be a clown.

CHARLIE: Same thing!

MOODY: I'd like to work in government. But Mrs. Lynde says:

RACHEL: (*Pops on*) Only rascals succeed in politics!

MISS STACY: What about you, Gilbert?

GILBERT: (*Stands*) If I pass the entrance, I'll go off to Queen's for a year. Then on to Redmond University--if I make good grades--if my father can afford it-- (*Sinks back*) If--if--if!

DIANA: I can't go to Queen's. My mother believes "Home is woman's proper sphere."

ANNE: I'd love to earn my way teaching school. But isn't Queen's dreadfully expensive?

JOSIE: I don't have to worry about earning a living. But I'm not an orphan living on charity. (*She gets elbowed.*)

ANNE: It's no use hoping--I know I can't go.

MOODY: My folks can send me--if I pass the entrance--

but I'll probably flunk the history questions and be a failure.

MISS STACY: Remember, class--there's a whole week of exams in Charlottestown.

STUDENTS: (*Groaning*) OH NO!

RUBY: I'll die. I'll just die.

CHARLIE: Will you be here next year--Miss Stacy--to help us?

MISS STACY: To tell the truth, I thought about taking another school. (*CLASS groans*) But I've grown rather fond of my pupils here. So I'll see you through the exams and I'll tutor you! (*CLASS cheers*)

GILBERT: Miss Stacy, can we practice our parts for tomorrow?

MISS STACY: There's still time. Ruby, you rehearse the tableau.

JOSIE: (*With book*) I'll prompt *you*, Gilbert. (*STUDENTS line up across stage. Right to Left: GILBERT strikes the orator's pose, loudly proclaiming; JOSIE prompts; DIANA studies sheet music; RUBY and ANNE practice extravagant tableau postures; CHARLIE begins "Sailor Hornpipe;" while MOODY reads nearby.*)

GILBERT: (*As Miss Stacy nods approval*) "Half a league, half a league, half a league onward. All in the valley of death, rode the the six hundred--" (*Consults Josie*)

DIANA: (*As Miss Stacy marks time*) "Flow gently, sweet Afton among thy green braes. Flow gently, I'll sing thee a song in thy praise." (*Ends off key*)

CHARLIE: (*Drags Moody over*) Moody, this is a duet--not a solo! (*Miss Stacy joins boys to help with "Hornpipe"*)

ANNE: I'm Faith--with my hands clasped--like so--

RUBY: (*Kneels, arms out*) I'm Hope--with my eyes uplifted-- Josie, you're Charity! (*Josie stomps over, thrusts*

*out a palm.   As GILBERT resumes, JOSIE returns.
Simultaneously, the whole CLASS noisily performs. MARILLA
enters Up Right.   She walks across the front of the stage,
scowling. Performers slowly draw to a halt.)*

GILBERT: "Forward the Light Brigade. Charge for the
guns! he said: Into the valley of Death rode the six hundred--"

MISS STACY, MOODY, CHARLIE: (*Heartily pulling
imaginary rope. As MARILLA nears.*) Ho! Ho! Ho! (*Eyes
now focus on Miss Stacy. Her solo chant turns into a wail as
she discovers Marilla.*)

MISS STACY: Ho! Ho!--OOOH!!! (*Shrieks*) GOOD
AFTERNOON, MISS CUTHBERT!   We were--just
rehearsing-- (*Rings bell*) Class dismissed. (*STUDENTS retreat
in haste*)

ANNE: You're here because Miss Stacy caught me
reading BEN HUR--but I just had to know how the chariot race
turned out!

MARILLA: I'll speak to you at home! (*ANNE exits in
dread*)

MISS STACY: (*Offers seat*) Miss Cuthbert, I want Anne
to join my special class.

MARILLA: (*Sits*) Special class? What has she done now?

MISS STACY: I'm offering lessons after school--to
prepare students for Queen's Academy--

MARILLA: Anne's not going to Queen's.

MISS STACY: But Anne is a clever girl--with a wonderful
imagination.

MARILLA: She gets to day dreaming and forgets her
duties.

MISS STACY: Miss Cuthbert, Anne has a genuine talent
for writing.

MARILLA: I think it's stuff and nonsense, but Mathew

dotes on every word.

MISS STACY: I think Anne belongs at Queen's, Miss Cuthbert.

MARILLA: (*Evasive*) Well--I don't know--about money and such-- Besides, the exam's more than a year away--

MISS STACY: In my opinion, it's always best to start early.

MARILLA: I'll think it over. (*Crosses*) Will that be all, Miss Stacy?

MISS STACY: (*Stops her*) Miss Cuthbert, have you considered Anne's future?

MARILLA: She'll always have a home at Green Gables. With Mathew and me.

MISS STACY: Always is a long time. . . anything can happen.

MARILLA: (*Considers*) Yes, it is an uncertain world. . . I've learned that.

MISS STACY: Shouldn't a girl be fitted out to earn a living?

MARILLA: Maybe so. Good afternoon, Miss Stacy. (*Exits*) Lord, those puffed sleeves look big as balloons!

(*LIGHTS UP in kitchen: MATHEW dozes in rocker. ANNE studies.*)

ANNE: (*At table*) Mathew?

MATHEW: (*Stirs, yawns*) Yes?

ANNE: Can you help me find the lowest common denominator?

MATHEW: Haven't they found that yet? They were looking for it when I was a boy.

ANNE: Geometry's my Waterloo. Even Diana does

better. And Gilber--I mean--some of the others--are so smart.

MATHEW: It'll come to you in time. You'll get the hang of it.

ANNE: Except for geometry, Miss Stacy and I are kindred spirits. When she says my name I feel instinctively that she adds an E!

MATHEW: Heard over at Blair's Store you were a good scholar.

ANNE: Today at school they applauded my recitation. (*Performs*) "Come into the garden, Maud, for the black bat, Night, has flown." (*Flapping arms*)

MATHEW: You'll have to say it all for me sometime-- (*She starts over*) Out--out in the barn.

ANNE : Life is more interesting now that I'm grown up. But it's a solemn thing to be almost fourteen. Everybody's talking about the entrance exam.

MATHEW: You'll need more school than Avonlea by and by. Would you like to go to Queen's and be a teacher?

ANNE: No point in dreaming--it cost Mr. Andrews hundreds for Prissy.

MATHEW: Hope I'm not putting my oar in if I tell you-- Marilla and me talked it over. We'll send you to Queen's--if you like--

ANNE: (*Thrilled*) Oh Mathew, I'll study extra hard! (*Kneels at rocker*) But don't expect too much in geometry!

MATHEW: (*Arm around her*) You'll beat out the whole Island!

ANNE: I am the best writer in class. That's not boasting-- Miss Stacy said so. I just love Miss Stacy. Don't you?

MATHEW: (*Shy*) Well, now--

ANNE: Marilla thinks her puffed sleeves are too fancy for a school teacher. (*Tragic*) But I know what it is to yearn for puffed sleeves.

MATHEW: (*Puzzled*) Puffed sleeves?

ANNE: The new fashion. Marilla says they look like watermelons--but all the girls have puffed sleeves.

MATHEW: (*To Audience*) Been noticing Anne don't dress like the others. Need to work on that.

ANNE: Mathew, did you ever go courting?

MATHEW: Well now. . . no. . . I never did.

ANNE: I'm sure Marilla never had a beau! (*Bundled up, DIANA enters Left, dashes into Cuthbert house.*)

DIANA: Anne! Anne!

ANNE: Oh, Diana. Has your mother relented at last?

DIANA: Minnie May is awful sick--she's got the croup. Mother and Father went to the political rally at Charlottestown-

ANNE: Marilla's gone too--with Mrs. Lynde--

DIANA: Oh Anne, I'm so scared.

MATHEW: (*Getting coat*) I'll harness Pearl and go for Dr. Stevens.

DIANA: (*Frightened*) Maybe Dr. Stevens has gone off too--

MATHEW: Then I'll go on to White Sands for Dr. Crane. (*Exits*)

DIANA: What if everybody's at the rally?

ANNE: Don't despair, Diana--I know all about the croup. Looking after three sets of twins gives you tons of experience.

DIANA: (*Frantic*) Minnie Mae's much worse and I used up the whole bottle of medicine!

ANNE: Put more wood on the stove. Keep all the kettle boiling.

DIANA: Tell me she's not going to choke.

ANNE: Hurry, Diana. Steam might ease the congestion. I'll be right over. (*DIANA races out; wrapped in shawl, ANNE follows*) What if Mathew has to drive to White Sands--that could take hours!

(*LIGHTS UP in kitchen: MARILLA and MRS. BARRY are talking.*)

MRS. BARRY: Marilla, it was dawn before Dr. Crane walked through the door. (*Sits*)

MARILLA: Anne was so tuckered out she stayed home from school.

MRS. BARRY: By then, Minnie Mae was fast asleep in her own bed.

ANNE: (*Enters*) Good afternoon, Mrs. Barry.

MRS. BARRY: Hello, Anne. . . . (*Uneasy pause*)

MARILLA: I'll just--get some--potatoes from the pantry. (*Exits*)

MRS. BARRY: The doctor said you saved my baby's life last night.

ANNE: Never thought I'd be glad Mrs. Hammond had three sets of twins!

MRS. BARRY: Anne, I'm sorry about that currant wine business. I see now you never intended to make Diana drunk. Will you forgive me?

ANNE: I accept your apology--with grace and humility.

MRS. BARRY: (*A take*) Good. (*Rises*) Because I want you and Diana to be friends.

ANNE: You are looking at a perfectly happy person, Mrs. Barry. In spite of my red hair!

MRS. BARRY: (*Embrace*) How can I ever repay you?

ANNE: No need, Mrs. Barry. Henceforth, I shall cover the past with a mantle of oblivion.

MRS. BARRY: (*Departs*) Then we'll expect you tonight

for dinner.

ANNE: (*Leaps for joy*) How stupendous! How simply incredibly stupendous!

MRS. BARRY: (*Crosses home*) Her speech is peculiar! (*To Audience*) Though certainly. . . lady-like. (*Exits*)

ANNE: Nobody ever used their best china on my account before! After dinner Diana and I made taffy but I let the pot burn. When we set the taffy out to cool, a cat walked across the plate. Nevertheless, tonight was an epoch in my life! (*Quick BLACKOUT*)

(*LIGHTS UP in kitchen: CUTHBERTS engage in heated discussion.*)

MATHEW: (*In rocker*) Well now, Marilla--it's a special occasion--

MARILLA: I don't approve of youngsters getting up concerts--running off to practices-- They ought to be home studying!

MATHEW: I think you should let Anne go to that concert tonight.

MARILLA: Well, I don't! (*Picks up sewing. ANNE enters to wash dishes--her back to audience.*)

MATHEW: (*Pleads*) It's a school concert, Marilla. It's Christmas.

MARILLA: Christmas or no Christmas, I don't believe in young folks staying out all hours. Anne, don't be sloshing that greasy dish-water over the entire kitchen.

MATHEW: (*Buckles overshoes*) The other girls are going.

MARILLA: And I'm surprised at Mrs. Barry for allowing Diana! (*Puts down sewing*) Can hardly see to darn these days. Must need glasses.

MATHEW: I think you're making a mistake, Marilla.

MARILLA: Mathew, who's bringing up this child, you or me?

MATHEW: (*Crosses for coat*) Well, now--you.

MARILLA: (*Stands*) Then don't interfere!

MATHEW: Ain't interferring to have an opinion. And my opinion is--

MARILLA: (*Battles*) You'd let Anne go to the moon, if she took the notion! But it's my duty to teach this waif-of-the-world manners and deportment--

MATHEW: (*Loud*) I still think you ought to let her go! Her heart's set on it!

MARILLA: (*Roar*) *Then she can go*!   Since nothing else will please you. (*MATHEW beams at jubilant ANNE, exits to barn.*)

ANNE: Oh Marilla, say those blessed words again!

MARILLA: Once is enough! This is Mathew's doings--I wash my hands of it.

ANNE: Mathew understands me. (*Wildly swinging wet dish cloth*) It's so nice to be understood.

MARILLA: Anne, you're dripping greasy water all over the floor! Never saw such a careless child.

ANNE: I'm a such a problem to you--always making mistakes. But think of the mistakes I don't make!

MARILLA: (*After a pause*) I'm thinking.

ANNE: I know you're trying to bring me up proper--which is very discouraging work--and I'll be (*another swing*) forever grateful--

MARILLA: Anne, you're dripping that filthy water--

ANNE: (*Wipes floor*) Sorry--just so excited--never been to a concert in my whole life. Let alone performed in one!

MARILLA: All I hope is you behave yourself.

ANNE: Diana's going to sing a solo. And I have my very own recitation! Though I need to practice the groaning. (*Crosses out with agonized comic groan*)

MARILLA: Anne! (*Still groaning, Anne exits to closet*) I'll be glad when all this fuss is over! Her head's stuffed full of dialogues--tableaus--and Lord knows what. (*Another horrendous groan. SHE exits shaking head. FADE*)

(*LIGHTS UP RIGHT: MATHEW timidly crosses yard, hiding gift.*)

MATHEW: (*Sings*) "God rest ye merry gentlemen. . . . (*Enters back door*)

ANNE: (*Enters from hall*) Merry Christmas, merry Christmas! Mathew, isn't it a lovely Christmas? I'm so glad it's white. (*MATHEW presents large box.*)

ANNE: Why, Mathew-- (*Opens gift*)

MATHEW: It's a Christmas present for you, Anne.

ANNE: Oh, Mathew! (*Revealing top of dress*)

MATHEW: It's the new way--the sleeves--

ANNE: (*Overcome*) Oh, Mathew!

MATHEW: Anne--don't you like it? Well now--

ANNE: (*Near tears*) Like it! Mathew--it's perfectly exquisite--a dream come true-- (*Embrace*)

MARILLA: (*Enters with small box, glares at dress*) I knew he was up to some foolishness. Been grinning like a cat for two weeks.

ANNE: Look at those beautiful sleeves!

MARILLA: (*Checks*) Enough material in those sleeves to make a blouse.

ANNE: I feared puffed sleeves would go out before I ever got any. I simply must try this on.

MARILLA: See that you take good care of it.

ANNE: (*Simply*) I always plan to be a model girl. But temptations get in my way! (*Carries dress to closet*)

MARILLA: Mathew, I made three warm, wearable dresses for the fall.

MATHEW: No harm in letting her have one pretty dress, Marilla.

MARILLA: You pamper her vanity. She's vain as a peacock now.

MATHEW: (*Smug*) She'll look prettier than the all rest--

MARILLA: (*Fumbles with box*) I--I bought Anne new patent shoes. They'll look right smart with that dress.

MATHEW: (*Grinning, sits in rocker*) That'll please her, Marilla.

MARILLA: New patents can't make her any more vain than she is already.

MATHEW: I'm awful proud of Anne and don't mind saying so.

MARILLA: (*Grudging*) I admit Anne's more steady and reliable. I'm even getting used to her constant chatter.

MATHEW: (*To Audience*) That's Marilla's way of saying she likes it.

MARILLA: At times I think she's actually outgrown her addlepated ways. Then she invents some new piece of *disaster*. (*FADE*)

(*LIGHTS UP DOWNSTAGE: From Right, GIRLS push small, flat-bottomed boat across stage. Boat rolls on wheels.*)

RUBY: Don't get too close to the water, Anne. You'll get your feet wet.

ANNE: I wish I was born in the days of Camelot. It's so romantic.

DIANA: You be Elaine. I haven't the courage to float down the river.

RUBY: Me neither. I could never pretend I was dead--I'd die of fright.

ANNE: A red-haired individual cannot be a lily maid! Ruby's Elaine.

RUBY: No! You're perfect, Anne.

DIANA: (*Invents*) Besides, your hair is much darker now.

ANNE: Honest? Do you think it could be called--auburn?

DIANA: (*Ruby nudges*) Oh, certainly.

ANNE: (*Thrilled*) Then I shall be Lady Elaine!

RUBY: Get in the boat--I mean--(*romantic*) "the barge"--

DIANA: Are you sure it's proper to play-act like this? Mrs. Lynde says--

RACHEL: (*Pops on*) Play-acting is abominably wicked!

ANNE: (*Climbs in*) Camelot was hundreds of years ago-- before Mrs. Lynde was born. (*Leans back, propped on pillows*)

RUBY: Elaine shouldn't talk when she's lying dead in her funeral barge.

Covering) Here, Mother's piano scarf--all I could find.

DIANA: (*Presents flower*) I don't have a lily--will an iris do? (*An arm reaches up for flower*)

RUBY: (*Reads from book, soulful*) First, we must kiss her quiet brow--

DIANA: (*Mournful*) Then I say--(*checks book*) sorrowfully as possible--"Sister, farewell forever." (*ANNE sits up for kiss*)

RUBY: (*Awed, copies Diana*) "Farewell, sweet sister." (*Kiss*)

DIANA: Smile a bit, Anne. It says here, "Elaine lay as

though she smiled." That's better.

RUBY: (*Girls push boat off*) Anne makes a wonderful Elaine. I'd be so nervous--

DIANA, RUBY: (*As boat disappears Left*) Farewe-e-l-l-l.

DIANA: I'd be afraid of drifting out too far.

RUBY: Why is she standing up!

DIANA: OH NO!

RUBY: (*Screams*) The barge is sinking! The barge is sinking!

DIANA: And we left the oars back at the landing--

RUBY: (*Screams*) She'll drown! She'll drown!

DIANA: The boat's sailing around the bend--

RUBY: (*Screams*) HELP! HELP!

DIANA: The boat's going under--

DIANA, RUBY: (*Racing off Left, screaming*) ANNE! ANNE!

(*STAGE RIGHT: ANNE is carried on by GILBERT. Bedraggled, wrapped in a piano scarf, ANNE wears one shoe and clutches another.*)

ANNE: Gilbert Blythe! I am quite able-bodied! Please put me down.

GILBERT: Gladly. (*Noisily dumps her to ground*) And I promise never to rescue you again! Just tell me what happened, Anne.

ANNE: (*Embarrassed*) We were playing Camelot. (*Rises*)

GILBERT: (*Smiles*) I think that scarf looks better on Ruby Gillis' piano.

ANNE: For your information, it's supposed to be a coverlet of gold!

GILBERT: I still don't understand what you were doing on

that log piling.

ANNE: The boat began to leak. When I floated near the bridge I grabbed hold of a log piling--so slippery I almost fell in-

GILBERT: And that's when I rowed by. Luckily.

ANNE: Thank you, Gilbert. (*Shakes hands stiffly*) I'm very much obliged. (*Strides past*)

GILBERT: (*Grabbing an arm*) Look here, Anne. Can't we be friends? I'm sorry I made fun of your hair that time. It was only a joke. Besides, that was years ago. Let's be friends. Please?

ANNE: (*Tempted, but:*) I vowed never to befriend you, Gilbert Blythe!

GILBERT: Fine! I'll never ask you again, Anne Shirley! (*Angry, exits Left*)

ANNE: Fine with me too! (*Watches with regret*) I have so many different Annes in me. If there was just the one, life would be much easier. (*Perks up*) Though not half so interesting! (*RUBY and DIANA return Right; RUBY still in hysterics.*)

RUBY: (*Rushes past Anne in her frenzy*) HELP! HELP! HELP!

DIANA: Anne! We thought you drowned. We felt like murderers because--

RUBY: (*Wails*) Because we made you play Ela-a-aine!

ANNE: Ruby--please. I am quite recovered.

DIANA: But Anne--I saw the boat go down--

ANNE: I scrambled up one of those big logs--barely escaping a watery grave. Right then--Gilbert Blythe came along in Mr. Andrew's boat and brought me to land.

RUBY: (*Ecstacy*) Oh, how splendid! He rescued you! Oh, how romantic!

DIANA: Of course, you'll speak to him after this.

ANNE: I most certainly will not! And I don't ever want to hear the word "romantic" again! Here's the piano scarf. Hope your mother doesn't notice that rip.

RUBY: OHHHH NOOOOO. . . . (*Bawling, exits Left with DIANA*)

ANNE: (*Tromps home*) I must be born under an unlucky star--in my imagination, adventures end in a blaze of glory!

(*LIGHTS UP in kitchen: MATHEW sits in rocker. MARILLA washes dishes as ANNE enters.*)

MARILLA: Will you ever have any sense, Anne?

ANNE: I think my prospects of becoming sensible are brighter than ever. (*Crosses to bedroom, sits--putting on shoe*)

MARILLA: (*Calls*) I don't see how.

ANNE: Today I learned a valuable lesson: Avonlea is not Camelot!

MARILLA: Well, who would have thought!

ANNE: Today has cured me of being too romantic. You will see a great improvement in that respect.

MARILLA: (*Emphatic*) Well, I certainly hope so. (*Exits to pantry*)

MATHEW: (*Checks for Marilla, crosses to bedroom*) Anne. Don't give up your romance, Anne. A little is a good thing--not too much, of course. But keep a little. (*FADE. HE exits to yard with cap.*)

(*LIGHTS UP DOWNSTAGE: STUDENTS enter Left with pre-exam jitters.*)

RUBY: (*Pacing*) When I think about going to

Charlottestown for those horrid--horrid exams, I feel sick all over.

MOODY: (*Enters with stool*) Seven times zero is zero. Eight times zero is zero. Nine times zero-- (*Sits Down Center.*)

CHARLIE: Moody, what are you muttering?

MOODY: Multiplication tables. To steady my nerves. Otherwise, I'll forget everything I know.

GILBERT: (*As MISS STACY enters*) Miss Stacy, do you think we'll pass? The question haunts me.

MISS STACY: We'll find out soon enough--they'll print the results in the Charlottestown paper. (*Places seat Down Left*)

GILBERT: That could be humiliating.

JOSIE: It's not fair. If you flunk one part, you flunk the whole exam.

ANNE: If I fail geometry--I fail the whole test! (*Places stool Center*)

JOSIE: Geometry's easy. A child of ten could learn it.

ANNE: I memorize the propositions. But they change the letters on me.

RUBY: The arithmetic part has numbers a yard long!

CHARLIE: Prissy Andrews said they put in trick questions--to trip you up.

GILBERT: It's the Latin conjugations I worry about.

CHARLIE: What good's Latin anyway? (*Clowns*) Amo, amas, amat.

MOODY: (*Rises*) I know I'll fail English history. And disgrace my parents. I feel it in my bones. (*Slumps back morosely*)

RUBY: (*Still pacing*) I get so nervous during tests. Wish I had nerves of steel like you, Charlie. Nothing rattles you.

CHARLIE: It's just an exam. If I flunk--I'll try again next year. What good is worrying?

MOODY: At least worrying makes you feel like you're doing *something*!

GILBERT: The worst part is waiting for the pass list to come out.

RUBY: If only I could just wake up when it's all over.

ANNE: I am *not* superstitious. But I do wish my exam number wasn't thirteen.

JOSIE: (*Taunts*) Thirteen is a very unlucky number!

GILBERT: Prissy Andrews stayed up nights cramming before each test. I'd be sleepwalking.

MISS STACY: Class, promise you won't stay up late. Don't open a book. Go to bed and get a good night's rest. (*Stands, rings bell*) And best of luck in Charlottestown!

ANNE: (*Crosses Right; to Audience*) Last night I dreamt the pass list came out: Gilbert's name was at the top. And mine wasn't there at all!

MOODY: (*Exiting with stool*) Capital of Manitoba is Winnepeg. Capitol of Alberta is-- (*Panic*) Charlie--where's the capital of Alberta!

CHARLIE: Wherever you left it, Moody. (*Follows with Anne's stool*)

GILBERT: Can I walk home with you, Ruby?

RUBY: Only if you explain how fractions can be *improper*--

JOSIE: (*Tags along*) Hey Gilbert--wait for me! My father says Gilbert will come in first.

GILBERT: Thanks, Josie, but I just want to pass. (*To Audience*) Mainly I want to beat out Miss Anne Shirley!

RUBY: Gilbert, don't you just hate those French verbs?

GILBERT: (*Kneels*) Ruby, my jewel, *je vous aime*

beaucoup.

RUBY: (*Screams*) GILBERT!!! (*Laughing, GILBERT exits--a girl on each arm. ANNE watches.*)

ANNE: (*Envious*) Sometimes I wish I'd made up with Gilbert Blythe--when I had the chance. Oh well, who cares?

MISS STACY: (*Takes story from briefcase*) I wanted to talk to you, Anne.

ANNE: Miss Stacy, there will be other springs, but if I don't pass the entrance--I won't recover enough to enjoy them.

MISS STACY: Anne, you've studied hard--for months.

ANNE: Mrs. Lynde says--

RACHEL: (*Pops on*) Anne Shirley, the sun will rise tomorrow whether you pass geometry or not!

MISS STACY: That's true. Though not very consoling.

ANNE: I want desperately to pass high for Marilla and Mathew--especially Mathew--

MISS STACY: Then don't stay up studying. It will only confuse you.

ANNE: (*To Audience*) Mainly I want to beat out Mr. Gilbert Blythe!

MISS STACY: Anne, this new story is delightful. About real people--about something that could happen right here in Avonlea. No lords and ladies, castles and kings--

ANNE: (*Smiles*) No handsome knight charging forth on a coal-black steed.

MISS STACY: And you skippped all those fancy words.

ANNE: I guess short, plain words can be good too. Like you said.

MISS STACY: Anne, you have the makings of a fine writer. Think about it.

ANNE: There's so much to think about when you're growing up--

MISS STACY: (*Rises*) Come, I'll walk you part way.

ANNE: Because you only have one chance. If you don't do it right, there's no starting over.

MISS STACY: You're bound to succeed, Anne--if you hold fast to your dreams.

ANNE: Miss Stacy, isn't it wonderful to have ambitions?

MISS STACY: The moment you achieve one ambition, another will come popping up--gleaming in the distance. (*FADE. SHE exits with seat*)

(*LIGHTS UP DOWN RIGHT: MARILLA crosses to bench with knitting.*)

RACHEL: (*Enters Up Left*) Marilla, why weren't you at Ladies' Aid? We were finishing up the Missionary quilts.

MARILLA: Mathew had a bad spell with his heart. Though he's all right again now.

RACHEL: That's a mercy.

MARILLA: Mathew takes spells oftener these days. So I'm troubled. Doctor says he's to avoid excitement--

RACHEL: That's easy enough for Mathew.

MARILLA: And he mustn't do any heavy work. Might's well order Mathew not to breathe as not to work.

RACHEL: Heard anything yet about the Queen's exam? How do you suppose Anne came out?

MARILLA: Rachel Lynde, it's been three whole weeks and not a word!

RACHEL: If you want my opinion--which I'm sure you don't--that's what comes of having a liberal as Superintendent of Education!

DIANA: (*Dashes on with newspaper*) The pass list is out!

RACHEL: About time!

DIANA: Anne! Anne! The pass list is out! (*Hands paper to Marilla*) Father bought papers on the afternoon train--from Bright River--

ANNE: (*Dashes from Up Right*) Well?

DIANA: You and Gilbert tied for first. But your name leads the pack!

RACHEL: We're right proud of you, Anne! (*Sits*)

DIANA: The whole class passed. Every one.

ANNE: I'm dazzled. I don't know what to say--I never dreamed. . . . (*Mathew enters*) Mathew! I passed! I'm first. Or one of the first. Takes my breath away.

MATHEW: I knew you could do it! Said all along you'd beat 'em easy.

MARILLA: You've done pretty well, I must say.

RACHEL: Pretty well? She's done very well!

MATHEW: Said all along you'd be first on the Island!

DIANA: Let's tell Miss Stacy. (*GIRLS race off*)

RACHEL: (*Studies list with Marilla*) Ruby's half way up. Charlie, too.

MARILLA: Josie just scraped by. At the bottom.

MATHEW: First! My girl is first!

MARILLA: (*Proud*) Never thought she'd get over her feather-brained ways.

RACHEL: Anne's turned out real smart and I don't mind admitting it.

MARILLA: I expect she's vain enough as it is.

RACHEL: Gracious sakes! Moody MacPherson got a conditional in history! But at least he passed. Well, I'm on my way to the MacPhersons with the news. (*Charges off with paper*)

MATHEW: (*Sly smile*) Guess Miss Stacy didn't do so bad after all. Even though she is a woman.

MARILLA: Still think those puffed sleeves look ridiculous.

MATHEW: Well now. . . I kind of like them.

MARILLA: (*Sad*) Mathew . . . in a few months our Anne will be gone. Gone for good. I get lonesome just thinking about it.

MATHEW: Marilla, she'll be back home to visit. . . .

MARILLA: Won't be the same. Men can't understand about these things.

MATHEW: Well, I dunno. . . .

MARILLA: (*Crosses to kitchen; Mathew follows*) House will seem terrible quiet this winter. . . and empty. (*Changes subject*) And I still don't like Miss Stacy's puffed sleeves! (*FADE*)

(*LIGHTS UP: Simultaneous scenes. MATHEW reads in rocker. All dressed up, DIANA enters from closet with ANNE'S Christmas gown.*)

DIANA: I think you should wear the pink.

ANNE: (*Enters in camisole, bloomers*) What about the flowered muslin?

DIANA: The pink's soft and frilly--suits you much better.

ANNE: I hope so. (*DIANA helps with dress*) Thank you, Diana. (*A greyer MARILLA crosses to table, dons glasses for knitting.*)

DIANA: Those ladies from the hotel will sparkle tonight-- with their silks and diamonds. Wouldn't you like to be rich, Anne?

ANNE: We are rich. Look at the sea--all silvery in the moonlight. We couldn't enjoy it more if we had heaps of diamonds.

DIANA: I don't know--I think diamonds might be

comforting.

ANNE: I love this little room so much. Don't see how I'll manage without Green Gables when I go to Queen's next month.

DIANA: Don't talk about it--makes me miserable and I'm determined to have a good time this evening. Here, let me tie your sash.

ANNE: I've never worn my hair up before. That's a milestone.

DIANA: (*Teasing*) You mean: "An epoch in my life!" (*ANNE laughs. As DIANA arranges ANNE's hair, MATHEW reads the paper to Marilla.*)

MATHEW: Well now, I think that's quite an honor for our Anne!

MARILLA: What else does it say? Can hardly see to read even with glasses.

MATHEW: "Summer guests at White Sands Hotel are sponsoring a concert to benefit the Charlottestown Hospital. A dance will follow."

MARILLA: (*Impatient*) What's it say about Anne?

MATHEW: "Bessie and Clara Simpson from the Baptist choir. . . will perform a duet. . . Milton Clark of Newbridge, a violin solo. . . Winnie Blair of Carmody, a Scotch ballad . . . Anne Shirley of Avonlea will recite!"

MARILLA: No need to burst your buttons, Mathew.

MATHEW: (*To Audience*) Marilla's just as pleased but won't admit it!

MARILLA: Still don't think it's proper for young folks to be gadding over to the Hotel all on their own!

DIANA: (*In bedroom*) Are you nervous?

ANNE: Trembling.

DIANA: You were encored at the Christmas concert.

Everyone raved.

ANNE: That was a school program. This is for fancy summer tourists--

DIANA: What are you going to recite?

ANNE: "Maiden's Vow"--it's so pathetic. And I like to make people cry.

DIANA: I'm going to pin your braids up. And put a big bow right here.

ANNE: (*Holds flower*) This is the last rose from Mathew's garden--I saved it. Mathew loves white roses.

DIANA: At the Christmas concert, a silk rose fell from your hair. I remember because Gilbert tucked it in his pocket. Or am I not supposed to mention that name?

ANNE: I don't mind. (*Admits*) I've been sorry I acted so stuck-up.

DIANA: What if Gilbert asks you to dance tonight? Will you accept?

ANNE: (*Hopeful*) I don't know--I might--

DIANA: So the old rivalry is finally over?

ANNE: (*Smiles*) Maybe. . . .

DIANA: Tonight I'll probably end up with Moody stepping on my toes.

ANNE: Just think, Diana. By the time we're twenty you'll be married with a houseful of children. And I'll be off teaching in a country school somewhere in Nova Scotia.

DIANA: (*Dramatic*) I'd like to marry some dashing wicked young man and reform him! (*Matter of fact*) But it's not likely.

ANNE: Maybe we could be old maids together--and friends forever.

DIANA: I think I'll stay fifteen. Twenty sounds so old and grown up!

MATHEW: (*Crosses timidly to bedroom.*) Anne. Anne.

ANNE: Mathew--come in--

MATHEW: (*Takes small box from pocket*) Well now, this is for you, Anne.

ANNE: Oh Mathew-- (*Opens box; MARILLA tiptoes over to peek in*)

MATHEW: (*Shy*) Bought those in town yesterday.

ANNE: (*Holds up necklace*) A string of pearls!

MATHEW: You'll be wanting them now, I expect.

ANNE: How lovely! (*Hug*) Oh thank you, Mathew. (*Grinning, MARILLA slips back as MATHEW smugly returns to rocker.*)

DIANA: Let me-- (*Assists with pearls*)

ANNE: Let those fine ladies sparkle with diamonds. I'd rather be Anne of Green Gables, wearing pearls that Mathew gave me--with more love than ever touched Milady's jewels.

DIANA: (*Helps*) And now for Milady's slippers.

ANNE: Am I ready?

DIANA: Anne, you look so stylish!

ANNE: Isn't it an amazing world? So many of my dreams have come true! (*Holding rose, a radiant ANNE whirls into kitchen.*)

DIANA: Well, what do you think of our star performer? (*MATHEW and MARILLA stare at this transformed ANNE.*)

ANNE: (*Anxious*) Is something wrong?

MATHEW: (*Awed*) No.

MARILLA: You look. . . neat and proper. I like your hair that way.

MATHEW: You look real nice, Anne.

MARILLA: That dress looks a mite thin for these damp nights.

ANNE: (*Kiss*) I'll be fine, Marilla. Good night, Mathew.

(*Kiss*)

MATHEW: My girl--the only one from Avonlea on the whole program!

CHARLIE: (*Offstage*) Come on, Anne! We'll be late!

ANNE: There's Charlie and Ruby--

DIANA: We've got to run-- (*GIRLS dash Right*)

ANNE: Bye.

MARILLA: (*From door*) Mind you keep your skirt clear of the wheel! (*Watches wistfully*) Almost wish I was going. .

MATHEW: She looked awful sweet.

MARILLA: (*Hiding her emotion*) Organdy's the most unserviceable stuff in the world--and I told you so when you bought it.

MATHEW: Well now. . . I kind of like it.

MARILLA: No use talking to you nowadays. If the clerks at Carmody store tell you a thing is fashionable, you plunk down your money.

MATHEW: You know, it's been a good arrangement after all.

MARILLA: What's that?

MATHEW: You raising up Anne strict and proper-like. (*Grins*) And me spoiling her now and again.

MARILLA: She's grown so fast. I'm going to miss her something terrible. (*Mustering control*) Expect she'll ruin that dress driving over in the dust! (*Exits to hall*)

MATHEW: (*Follows*) I'll bet she's encored! (*FADE*)

(*LIGHTS UP DOWNSTAGE: ANNE enters, crosses Center. Dance MUSIC.*)

ANNE: When I stood on stage. . . looking out at a sea of strange faces. . . my knees trembled, my heart fluttered.

Seeing those elegant ladies in rustling silks--my dress suddenly seemed so plain-- (*FRIENDS rush on Left, surrounding ANNE.*)

RUBY: That was wonderful, Anne. I cried like a baby.

MOODY: (*Worried*) At first I thought you forgot the words.

CHARLIE: Were you scared?

ANNE: Terrified. My voice wouldn't start!

RUBY: I'd die. An audience full of Mr. and Mrs. Money-Bags!

ANNE: I reached up. . . (*Touches pearls*) and took courage somehow--

RUBY: Your voice was so--so dramatic!

MOODY: Honest, Anne--you were the best thing on the show.

CHARLIE: Lots better than those ladies from the Baptist choir.

DIANA: Anne, you were the only one encored! (*Waltz MUSIC up.*)

RUBY: I'd like to be Mrs. Money-Bags. Wouldn't you?

ANNE: (*Joyous*) I don't want to be anyone but myself!

CHARLIE: (*Pushing Moody aside, bows to Ruby*) Mr. Charles Money-Bags, Esq. requests the honor of this dance. (*They waltz off*)

MOODY: (*Bashfully taps shoulder*) Anne--

GILBERT: (*Enters*) Hello, Anne. (*Crosses in; MOODY backs off*)

ANNE: (*Smiles eagerly*) Hello, Gilbert. (*About to invite Anne, GILBERT stands uncomfortably.*)

GILBERT: (*Turns suddenly*) Diana, would you care to dance? (*With a surprised glance to Anne, DIANA spins away.*)

ANNE: (*To Audience*) We might have been good friends--

(*More hopeful, MOODY summons his courage and taps Anne.*)

MOODY: Anne, if I try not to step on your toes, will you dance with me? Gee, thanks. (*Dancing off*) Sorry--ooops-- Sorry. (*ANNE groans*) I'm sorry! (*More groans. DANCERS stumble off Left; LADIES enter Right, crossing.*)

MRS. BARRY: Anne's a credit to Avonlea and no mistake.

RACHEL: I don't approve of play-acting. But recitation-- nothing sinful about that.

MRS. BARRY: At first I thought Anne would never get started. But she calmed down and sailed clear through.

RACHEL: If you want my opinion--which I'm sure you don't--that Winnie Blair sings like a sick rooster. Only reason she got picked is 'cause her brother's on the committee. Did you hear about the new lawyer's wife?

MRS. BARRY: (*All ears*) No--what?

RACHEL: Julia Barry--you should have seen the dress she wore last week! (*Crosses past*) The neckline started up in Nova Scotia and went clear down to South America!! (*Exits Left*)

MRS. BARRY: (*Follows*) Gracious Providence! Of all unaccountable things! Did ever any mortal! (*FADE*)

(*LIGHTS UP DOWNSTAGE: Train Whistle. STATION MASTER enters*)

STATION MASTER: (*With clipboard*) All aboard! Good afternoon, Mr. Cuthbert--

MATHEW: (*Enters, crossing Left with suitcase*) Is that the train for Charlottestown?

STATION MASTER: About to pull out, Mr. Cuthbert.

MARILLA: (*Enters*) Anne! Anne--don't be dawdling.

That child gets into such a fluster--I thought she'd never get packed! Anne!

STATION MASTER: All aboard! All aboard! (*Blows whistle*)

ANNE: (*Runs on*) Marilla, thanks for putting flounces on my skirts. I can study better with fashionable clothes.

MARILLA: You be sure to write once a week, like you promised.

ANNE: Queen's is so far away. I'll feel like a cat in a strange garret.

MATHEW: Well now, you'll do just fine.

ANNE: I'll make you proud of me, Mathew.

MATHEW: (*Hugs*) I'm already proud of you, Anne.

STATION MASTER: Best be getting on, Miss.

MARILLA: Eat proper, keep your room tidy, finish your studies, and-- (*Turns, taking hanky from purse*)

ANNE: What's wrong, Marilla?

MARILLA: (*Wipes tears*) Cinders from the train I guess. I was thinking of the little girl you used to be, Anne.

ANNE: I'm not a bit changed--not really.

MARILLA: (*Sniffles*) Look at you: All grown up now--so tall and stylish--seems as if you don't belong in Avonlea anymore.

ANNE: (*Rushed*) Marilla! The true me--down deep--is just the same. And I'll love you and Mathew and dear Green Gables every day of my life! (*Takes suitcase. Train whistle. ANNE dashes out.*)

MATHEW, MARILLA: (*Waving*) Goodbye, Anne.

STATION MASTER: Sure has changed from when I first saw that girl--years ago--sitting on her suitcase--looking so forlorn. (*Exits. Another whistle. SOUND of train pulling out.*)

MARILLA: (*Teary*) Wish she could haved stayed that little

girl—even with all her peculiar ways.

MATHEW: Well now, I guess she ain't been much spoiled. I guess putting my oar in occasional never did much harm after all.

MARILLA: I suppose not.

MATHEW: She's smart and pretty, and loving too, which is better than all the rest. She's been a blessing to us.

MARILLA: (*Weeps*) Those trains put out a terrible lot of cinder, if truth be told.

MATHEW: Reckon there never was a luckier mistake—

MARILLA: That was no mistake. It was Providence. (*Takes his arm*) We needed her, Mathew. (*Arm in arm, THEY return home.*)

(*LIGHTS UP DOWNSTAGE: RUBY and JOSIE enter Up Left. In a dreamy mood, ANNE follows, stands apart.*)

RUBY: (*Crosses Right with tin box*) Here's a quiet spot, Anne.

JOSIE: What did Marilla send this time? I'm starving.

RUBY: Mmmm . . . brownies.

JOSIE: I figured Marilla would load you up with something scrumptious.

ANNE: (*Wistful*) About now, Mathew would be coming home. Marilla would be at the gate waiting for him. And moonlight would be falling on the orchard. . . .

JOSIE: (*Gobbles brownie*) Don't tell me you're still homesick!

RUBY: Aren't you?

JOSIE: (*Taking a handful*) Some people have no self-control. I could never be homesick. Not for poky old Avonlea.

(*Crosses to bench*)

RUBY: My French professor is a doll. His moustache would make your heart flutter.

JOSIE: Ruby, hand over the brownies! I'm hungry as a bear.

RUBY: (*Crosses; Josie snatches tin*) Gilbert's gotten so serious. I don't understand half the things he says--reminds me of you, Anne, when you take a thoughtful fit. (*Sits*)

JOSIE: Professor Tremain thinks Gilbert is sure to win the Gold Medal for "academic excellence." And Emily Clay will take the Silver.

RUBY: Maybe you could try for a medal, Anne.

ANNE: (*Turns, smiling*) It would please Mathew, I'm sure. Next to trying and winning--I guess the best thing is trying and failing.

RUBY: Failing! (*Stands*) I should be studying. My horrid old Latin prof gave us twenty lines to memorize for tomorrow.

JOSIE: (*Stands*) What are you girls going to wear for commencement? I've got my dress all picked out. Gilbert loves blue.

RUBY: Gilbert's been walking me home from class. But honestly, I think Frank Stockley is lots more fun.

JOSIE: How come Gilbert walks you? He never carries my books!

ANNE: (*Whispers softly*) Gilbert. . . .

RUBY: I like Gilbert all right. (*Crosses past Anne*) And Frank. And Charlie and Bill and Gregory. And Donald. (*Turns*) What about you, Anne? Anne!

ANNE: Oh--I was just thinking about--my essay--for composition class.

JOSIE: (*Crosses to her*) I've been wondering, Anne. Do people with that red hair ever get used to it?

RUBY: Josie! (*Exits Left–JOSIE in tow*)

ANNE: (*To Audience*) I've made a heroic effort to like that person. But Josie Pye will not be liked! (*SHE Follows. FADE*)

(*LIGHTS UP in kitchen: MARILLA writes to Anne.*)

MARILLA: Doesn't seem possible school is nearly over. Buds are out on the chestnut trees and the apple orchard's waiting for you. Hope you can read this--my eyes still trouble me. Mathew's been frail, I'm sorry to say. You'll cheer him up when you come home. Naturally, Mathew thinks you'll be coming home with that Gold Medal. . . . (*FADE kitchen*)

(*LIGHTS UP DOWNSTAGE: ANNE enters Left reading letter. RUBY and JOSIE follow. Anne's line overlap Marilla's.*)

ANNE: ". . . coming home with that Gold Medal." Ruby, I do so want to win. For Mathew's sake.

RUBY: Aren't you excited? I am. In one moment we'll know: whether it's you or Gilbert!

ANNE: Be a dear and check the bulletin board for me. I haven't the heart to look.

OFFSTAGE VOICES: HIP HIP HURRAY! HURRAY FOR GILBERT!

RUBY: Sorry, Anne.

ANNE: (*Downcast*) Poor Mathew will be so disappointed.

JOSIE: I knew Gilbert would win. Professor Tremain said--(*BOYS noisily enter with GILBERT on their shoulders.*)

RUBY: (*Shaking*) Congratulations!

ANNE: (*Shaking*) Congratulations, Gilbert!

GILBERT: Congratulations to you, Anne Shirley! (*Leaps down*)

ANNE: (*Bewildered*) Me?

GILBERT: You won the Avery Scholarship!

MOODY: Board of Governors granted an Avery scholarship! To a student from Queen's Academy. First time ever!

CHARLIE: To the student writing the best essay: You!

GILERT: That means four years at Redmond University.

RUBY: What about our exams?

CHARLIE: We passed, Ruby!

RUBY: (*Jumps up screaming*) I passed! I passed!

MOODY: Hurray for Anne!

CHARLIE: Three cheers for Avonlea: HIP HIP--

STUDENTS: HURRAY!

CHARLIE: HIP HIP--

STUDENTS: HURRAY!

CHARLIE: HIP HIP--

STUDENTS: (*CHARLIE and MOODY raise up Anne*) HURRAY!

MOODY: We all passed. Except you, Josie. You flunked the whole year! (*With Anne shoulder high, STUDENTS exit Left*)

JOSIE: (*Shouts*) Who wants to teach at some boring little country school? My father can afford to send me back to Queen's!

RUBY: (*Hesitant*) Josie--can I borrow that blue dress your father bought? (*JOSIE stomps Left; RUBY shrugs to audience, follows*)

(*LIGHTS UP in kitchen: MATHEW enters with bucket.*)

MARILLA: (*At table*) Can hardly believe Anne's finally home for a spell. Longest winter I ever put in--

MATHEW: (*Smug smile*) Reckon you're glad we kept her, Marilla?

MARILLA: You don't have to rub it in, Mathew. (*Exits to hall. Stooped, MATHEW slowly crosses yard. ANNE enters Left.*)

ANNE: Mathew! Mathew! (*HE stops*) I've had such a wonderful morning, roaming through the woods hunting up my old dreams. Sit down for a moment, Mathew. I've missed talking to you.

MATHEW: My girl! Earned a first-class teacher's license and an Avery Scholarship! (*Sits*)

ANNE: You look tired, Mathew. You've been working too hard.

MATHEW: I'm getting old. Just keep forgetting it.

ANNE: Why don't you take things easier?

MATHEW: Well now, I can't seem to. Guess I've worked hard all my days and would rather drop in the harness.

ANNE: If only I'd been the boy you ordered. I could have spared you a hundred ways. You wouldn't have had to work so hard--if I'd been a boy--

MATHEW: Well now, I'd rather have you than a dozen boys, Anne. Just remember that--more than a dozen boys. (*Rises*) Reckon it wasn't a boy that took the Avery scholarship, was it? No. It was a girl--my girl--my girl that I'm so proud of.

ANNE: (*Kisses his cheek*) Oh, Mathew. I do love you. (*MATHEW smiles shyly, exits as DIANA hurries on.*)

DIANA: And how is my Anne with an E? (*THEY rush together*)

ANNE: Oh Diana, it's so good to be back again. To see

those pointed firs against the pink sky.   And that white
orchard-- And it's good to see you again, Diana.

DIANA: Josie Pye said you liked some new friend much
better than me.

ANNE: Josie is horrid as ever, and you are the dearest
friend in all the world. (*Embrace*)

DIANA: You've done so well, Anne. I suppose you
won't be teaching, now that you've won the Avery.

ANNE: I'll be going to Redmond University in September.
But first, three glorious months of summer.

DIANA: Ruby and Moody both found teaching jobs on the
Island. And Gilbert Blythe is going to teach, too.

ANNE: (*Disappointed*) Gilbert won't be going on to
Redmond?

DIANA: His father can't afford to send him. (*Tugging*)
Come on, Mother's dying to see you. And Minnie Mae. (*Exit*)

(*LIGHTS UP in kitchen: RACHEL and MARILLA enter
from pantry.*)

MARILLA: Help yourself to cake, Rachel. (*Pours tea;
RACHEL sits.*) Can't imagine what Mathew's up to. (*Exits*)

RACHEL: (*Samples*) Never one to brag, but my lemon
cake is moister.   Course, nowadays you can't buy decent
baking powder--it's all adulterated. If you want my opinion--
which I'm sure you don't--the government's to blame.

MARILLA: (*Returns*) Rachel--Rachel--Mathew's fainted!
On the bedroom floor!

RACHEL: I'll try the smelling salts. (*Finds bottle, races
out*)

MARILLA: Anne! Anne!   (*ANNE runs in from yard*)

Fetch the buggy and go for Dr. Stevens.   Hurry now--
Mathew's fainted.   (*ANNE dashes out; MARILLA starts for
hall*)
     RACHEL: (*Returning, stops her*) Marilla, I don't believe
we can do anything for him now.
     MARILLA: Rachel--you don't think--   (*Rachel nods;
Marilla desperately clutches her*) Mathew--oh no--   (*Quick
BLACKOUT*)

     (*DOWNSTAGE: DIM LIGHTING for funeral scene. In
     a short black cape, ANNE crosses Down Right, stands
     alone.*)

     ANNE: (*To Audience, calm*) Dr. Stevens said death was
instantaneous and probably painless. Can't seem to realize it.
Keep thinking if I go to the barn, Mathew will be there. . .
waiting for me. . . .   And I can't even cry--just have this
horrible ache, here.

     (*In a simple, ceremonial procession, FRIENDS solemnly
     enter Left. DIANA with MRS. BARRY and MOODY;
     GILBERT, MISS STACY, STATION MASTER. One at
     a time, THEY step forward in formal fashion, then
     return. YOUNGSTERS are ill at ease.*)

     MOODY: (*Crosses to Anne, nervous*) "Please. . . accept
. . . my sincere condolences."   (*Steps back*)
     DIANA: (*With a nudge from MRS. BARRY, crosses*)
Anne, would you like to spend the night with me?
     ANNE: Thank you, Diana.   But I need to be here--with
Marilla. I still can't believe it.
     DIANA: I understand. (*Embrace; steps back. Black shawl*

We're also considering the Evans place. (*An afterthought, turns*) Oh--and Mabel sends her sympathy--of course.

MARILLA: (*Alone*) Never thought I'd live to see the day I'd sell my home.

ANNE: (*Enters from house*) Who was that driving off?

MARILLA: Mr. Spencer heard I was selling Green Gables and wants to buy it.

ANNE: Marilla, you don't mean to sell Green Gables?

MARILLA: Wish I didn't have to. If my eyes were better, I might stay on. But I may lose my sight altogether.

ANNE: Marilla, I couldn't live without Green Gables.

MARILLA: Place won't bring much--but I'll manage. And you've got your scholarship.

ANNE: Nothing could be worse than losing Green Gables. Nothing.

MARILLA: (*Distressed*) Can't stay here alone--I'd go crazy with trouble and loneliness.

ANNE: (*Crosses to bench*) But you won't stay here alone. I'm not going to the University!

MARILLA: Not going! Whatever are you talking about!

ANNE: I can use my scholarship later. It's all figured out. Mr. Barry wants to rent the farm and I'm going to teach--the trustees say I can have the school at White Sands.

MARILLA: (*Crosses*) I can't let you give up everything. What an idea!

ANNE: After all you've done for me?

MARILLA: Fiddlesticks.

ANNE: I needed you once, Marilla. Now you need me. It's all settled. I'm sixteen and a half and my mind is made up!

MARILLA: I still don't feel I should let you give up your future.

ANNE: (*Rises*) I have my future unrolling before me--it's

just taking a new turn. Nobody could love Green Gables the way I do--the way you do. So we must keep it.

MARILLA: Oh, you blessed girl. (*Embrace*)

RACHEL: (*Arriving*) Just saw Mr. Spencer driving off--

MARILLA: (*To Audience*) I knew she'd be right over.

RACHEL: Is it true--is Mr. Spencer buying Green Gables?

ANNE: No such thing. Green Gables is not for sale.

MARILLA: Anne's not going to Redmond.

RACHEL: That's a relief. I don't believe in women cramming their heads full of Latin and Greek and all that nonsense.

ANNE: I'll study all that nonsense by correspondence.

MARILLA: She's taking a teaching position.

RACHEL: A good thing too. If you want my opinion--which I'm sure you don't--women nowadays are getting far too ambitious.

ANNE: I still have my ambitions--strong as ever! I'm going to write--though not about castles filled with lovesick princesses--

MARILLA: (*Teasing*) No more Cordelias?

ANNE: I'm going to write about the people I know and love. Like Miss Stacy said. I'm going to write about plain old Avonlea.

RACHEL: Well, I could give you an earful, that's sure and certain.

MARILLA: I expect so, Rachel.

RACHEL: I remember the first time I set eyes on you, Anne. Lawful heart, I'll never forget that tantrum!

ANNE: (*Chagrined*) Neither will I.

RACHEL: I said, "Marilla Cuthbert will rue the step she took." But I was mistaken. And no wonder--an odder child there never was.

MARILLA: Isn't that the truth!

RACHEL: And it's nothing short of wonderful how she's turned out. Especially in looks!

ANNE: (*Laughs*) I don't know what happened to those freckles.

RACHEL: (*Looks off Left*) Bless my soul! What's Gilbert doing out this way? Which reminds me--I hear they've given Avonlea school to Gilbert Blythe!

MARILLA: (*To Audience*) Count on Rachel for the latest news.

GILBERT: (*Crossing in*) Good afternoon, Miss Cuthbert. Mrs. Lynde. I'd like to talk to you, Anne. (*THEY stand awkwardly. RACHEL beams, gawking with curiosity.*)

MARILLA: (*Drags her away*) Rachel, you wanted to see my new skirt pattern.

RACHEL: (*Struggles to peer back*) What skirt pattern, Marilla?

GILBERT: Anne, the trustees voted to give you Avonlea school.

ANNE: But I thought they promised Avonlea to you.

GILBERT: I withdrew my application. And suggested your name instead. I knew you'd be wanting to stay and help Marilla.

ANNE: (*Crossing past him*) I can't let you do that--

GILBERT: I guess you can't stop me. I've already signed the papers at White Sands. So it wouldn't do any good to refuse.

ANNE: (*Turns*) I don't feel I ought to take it. Doesn't seem fair.

GILBERT: (*Moving closer*) I can be stubborn too, you know.

ANNE: Gilbert, I want to thank you. For giving up

Avonlea school.

GILBERT: (*Smiles*) You're finally forgiving me after all these years?

ANNE: I forgave you long ago, but was too proud to say so.

GILBERT: We were born to be friends, Anne. I only teased you because-

ANNE: Because?

GILBERT: Because--I thought you had wonderful red hair. (*Touches her hair*)

ANNE: (*Taking his hand*) We've been good enemies. Maybe now we can be good friends--

GILBERT: I guess we have a lot of catching up to do.

ANNE: I'd like that, Gilbert. (*Holding her hand, GILBERT moves Left. Parting, ANNE watches him go. Moving Center, ANNE kneels in POOL OF LIGHT.*)

ANNE: Mathew, we aren't going to lose Green Gables. I thought you'd want to know. I planted a rosebush by your grave today. A cutting from the one your mother brought over from Scotland. You always liked those white roses best. (*MATHEW enters Up Right, stands in the shadows, speaks softly.*)

MATHEW: You're my girl--I'd rather have you than a dozen boys. (*Motionless, ANNE listens to the gentle voices.*)

MARILLA: (*Enters kitchen*) I love you like you were my own flesh and blood.

DIANA: (*Enters Up Left*) You're odd but I think I like you.

MISS STACY: (*Enters Down Left*) You have a rare talent, Anne. Never forget that.

ANNE: (*Rises*) Dear old world. You are lovely. And I'm glad to be alive in you. (*Returning, GILBERT stands behind*

ANNE, hands on her shoulders.)
    GILBERT: Carrots. (*Tenderly kisses her cheek*)

(*LIGHTS DIM.*)

* * *

PRODUCTION NOTES

LIGHTING

The "lights up" cues in the script are intended to focus the attention of the reader. Lighting changes, in the main, should consist of quick cross fades as the lines of a scene end. The script mentions three blackouts; however, these should be momentary only. Continuity is the important issue.

SCENERY

The set, fragmentary and suggestive, consists of two rooms, bedroom and kitchen. These rooms can be conveyed through partial walls, or simply with window and door frames set against stage curtains. Practical window or doors are not necessary--these are openings only. The hall entrance leads to pantry; the closet allows for quick exits from the bedroom. In the original production, bedroom, closet, and hall openings were curtained.

The kitchen is furnished with table, chairs, a rocker facing down and an upstage counter for washing dishes. The simplest washing arrangement involves a large pan set on the counter top; a more elaborate arrangement includes a countertop with set-in sink and working water pump. Furnish the bedroom with small bed, vanity and chair.

The rooms can be set on a platform. The area downstage of house (and alongside) is flexible, transforming into various locales--with virtually no scenery required.

For seating, a Down Right bench or stepped platform is needed; the platform would also provide a playing area. This

Down Right area works for scenes in the Cuthbert yard, scene with the girls at Queen's, and apology scene at Rachel's. In addition to a blackboard which rolls on, the setting for the Phillips' school scene (Act One) is created with small stools which students carry on and off. The stools are lined up for the officious Mr. Phillips.

In contrast, for the first Miss Stacy scene, students sit casually around her on floor. The second Stacy scene can be done with two stools. For a teacher's seat, Miss Stacy sets a stool or small bench Down Left and exits with seat on fadeouts. Miss Stacy offers this seat to Marilla. A stepped platform Down Left would substitute for stools and teacher's seat in Act Two school scenes.

CHRONOLOGY

Though the dialogue identifies Anne's age progression, this summary may be helpful.

ACT ONE: ARRIVAL--June; Anne is 12 1/2. PICNIC-- that summer. SCHOOL/HAIR DYEING-- September. TEA SCENE--following June; Anne is 13 1/2. FALL FROM ROOF--summer.

ACT TWO: SCHOOL--October. SICK BABY-- November; Anne is "almost fourteen." CHRISTMAS CONCERT, CHRISTMAS DRESS--December. BOAT SCENE--following summer; Anne is 14 1/2. SCHOOL/EXAM--following May; Anne is 15 1/2. EXAM RESULTS, HOTEL CONCERT--summer; "I'd rather stay fifteen." TRAIN STATION--September.

QUEEN'S--fall.   GRADUATION--May.
HOMECOMING--June.   CONCLUSION--summer;
Anne is "sixteen and a half."

COSTUMES

A basic costume can be varied by adding shawls, cape:
aprons, pinafores, blouses, vests, etc.   More extensiv
costuming helps convey the passage of time. Also, Anne's ha
style changes as she grows up, evolving from pigtails, to sing
French braid, to hair up.   The following possibilities a
suggestions only.

ANNE--Because Anne is on stage so much, her costum
changes require planning. The following information shou
prove helpful even if different changes are planned.   Un
HOTEL scene, Anne wears plainer clothes than the other girl:

ACT ONE: ARRIVAL--faded, ill-fitting dress; lace-u
boots, black tights, bloomers. TANTRUM--Anne wea
arrival dress. NIGHTGOWN- Anne exits to closet wit
suitcase, puts nightgown on over her dress. Anne enters
nightgown: "We've decided on the experiment." If boo
show under nightie, Anne "unties" shoe as lights fad
Anne exits to closet, takes off gown. PICNIC DRESS
Anne exits to closet with new calico, enters in dress.

SCHOOL/HAIR DYEING--Anne continues in picnic dress
with apron or pinafore. For "green hair," spray an ol
blonde or red wig with green hair color--not spray paint
Anne enters with wig completely covered by huge kerchie
TEA SCENE--Anne wears slightly more attractive cotto

print. This is a fast change; time is needed to remove wig--
she can finish buttoning on entrance. FALL FROM
ROOF--same, with apron. During intermission, Anne
switches to lighter tights.

ACT TWO: SCHOOL--same dress with pinafore. There
is time for a change during Marilla's scene with Miss
Stacy. SICK BABY--simple two-piece cotton.
CHRISTMAS--add pinafore. BOAT SCENE--same two-
piece outfit; pull blouse out of skirt for disheveled look.
SCHOOL/EXAM--add pinafore. EXAM RESULTS--there
is time for a fast change.

HOTEL CONCERT--the effect here should be a wonderful
transformation (the old Ugly Duckling idea). Her dress--
finally with puffed sleeves--should be lovely but not gaudy.
Anne can wear the gown Mathew gave; the audience enjoys
seeing her in this dress. Adapt references to "pink" or
"organdy" if necessary. Add heels--these can be simple
pumps; period shoes are not necessary. To appear taller
and older, Anne wears heels and longer skirts for the rest
of the play.

TRAIN STATION--this is a fast change; the outfit here
becomes the basis for the funeral costume: Anne wears
long, dark plaid skirt, blouse, dark heels. QUEEN'S--add
jacket; GRADUATION--substitute vest for jacket;
HOMECOMING--take off vest; FUNERAL--add short
black cape. CONCLUSION--Anne wears a pretty,
summery dress for the remainder of the play; fast change.

MARILLA--To a few simple dresses or skirts and blouses, add

shawls, aprons, purses, hats, etc. A cape can be worn in SCHOOL and STATION scenes.   QUEEN'S--the costume Marilla wears while writing letter facilitates the switch to FUNERAL scene: Try a simple white or grey blouse, print skirt, and plaid apron. Take off apron for death scene. FUNERAL--fast change: Trade print skirt for black one, add black lace shawl. Minus shawl, this costume can be worn for remainder of play.

DIANA--Diana has a fast change after tea party if a plainer outfit is desired for farewell scene. Another fast change involves switch to ball gown, Act Two. Diana's wardrobe is finer than Anne's.

JOSIE--Josie wears somewhat fancier clothes than the other girls.

MATHEW--Though he appears initially in his Sunday suit, Mathew wears work clothes--overalls, boots, work shirts, warm jackets.

BOYS--Act One--knickers, suspenders, oxfords or boots, knee-high stockings, plaid or corduroy collarless shirts (ordinary shirts with collars tucked under will work). FALL FROM ROOF: add vests or sweaters. Act Two--SCHOOL/MISS STACY--same. BOAT SCENE--Gilbert can wear same shirt, new knickers and matching vest, cap. SCHOOL/EXAM-- suit pants, bow ties, wing tip shirts, suspenders. HOTEL CONCERT--suits,   new   bow   ties,   same   shirts. GRADUATION--same shirts and pants, dressier vests, bow ties. FUNERAL--suits. CONCLUSION--Gilbert switches to another vest.

PROPS

CLOTHING HOOKS--Wall hooks near back door are needed for Marilla's shawl, Anne's wrap, and Mathew's jacket and cap. If no walls are used, substitute a clothes tree.

SLATES--Inexpensive slates can be purchased at craft or hobby stores. Pre-break Anne's slate and glue it back together. The effect is wonderful--pieces fly. These pieces can be picked up by Mr. Phillips as he scolds Anne, and by Diana before her exit.

SEATING--Seven small stools are needed for students in Act One; these are carried on and off by the actors. Miss Stacy needs a small teacher's seat--bench or stool.

LOCK OF HAIR--Diana palms a bit of crepe hair which Anne slips out while "cutting" Diana's hair.

BROOCH--A brooch which clips is preferable to one which pins on. No need for an amethyst--the stone doesn't show.

*

PLAYING "CAMELOT" -- THE BOATLESS VERSION.

(RUBY and DIANA run on Down Right.)

RUBY: Don't get too close to the water, Diana. You'll get your feet wet.   *(Waves off Left)*

DIANA: *(Sorrowfully throwing kiss off Left)* "Farewell, sweet sister."

RUBY: *(Reads from book)* "Sister, farewell forever." Anne's right! Playing Camelot is ever so romantic!

DIANA: *(Calls, waving flower)* Anne, I forgot to give you the lily.

RUBY: Doesn't Anne make a wonderful Lady Elaine! I'd be so nervous.

DIANA: I don't have the courage to float down the river.

ANNE'S VOICE: I think the boat is leaking.

RUBY: Quiet, Anne!

DIANA: *(Calling)* Elaine shouldn't talk when she's lying dead in her funeral barge!

RUBY: I could never pretend I was dead--I'd die of fright.

DIANA: I'd be afraid of drifting out too far.

RUBY: Me too.

DIANA: Are you sure it's proper to play act like this? Mrs. Lynde says--

RACHEL: *(Popping on)* Play-acting is abominably wicked.

RUBY: *(In a panic)* Why is she standing up!

DIANA: Oh no!

RUBY: *(Screams)* The barge is sinking! The barge is sinking!

DIANA: And we left the oars at the landing--

RUBY: *(Screams)* She'll drown! She'll drown!

DIANA: The boat's sailing around the bend--

RUBY: (*Screams*) HELP! HELP!

DIANA: The boat's going under--

DIANA, RUBY: (*Running off Left, screaming*) ANNE! ANNE!

(*STAGE RIGHT: ANNE, wrapped in a piano scarf, bedraggled--wearing one shoe and clutching the other-- is carried on by GILBERT.*)

ANNE: Gilbert Blythe! I am quite able-bodied! Please put me down.

GILBERT: Gladly. (*Dumping her on ground*) And I promise never to rescue you again. Just tell me what happened?

ANNE: (*Embarrassed*) We were playing Camelot.

GILBERT: And you were Lady Elaine, I suppose.

ANNE: I told them a red-haired individual should not play the lily maid. But Ruby and Diana insisted.

GILBERT: I think that scarf looks better on Ruby Gillis' piano.

ANNE: For your information, it's supposed to be my coverlet of gold!

GILBERT: I still don't understand what you were doing on that log piling.

(*Scene continues as before.*)

*

IN JULIET'S GARDEN
Judy Elliot McDonald

Comedy / 7f, (1m optional) / Simple staging
Juliet Capulet invites four other heroines of Shakespeare's classics (Katharina, Portia, Ophelia and Desdemona) to lunch in her favorite garden in Verona to discuss 'issues' they all have with their plots. All the ladies have suggestions how these issues might be remedied. Shakespeare has also been invited, but instead sends an envoy, his literary agent and editor Jacqueline de Boys, who attempts to save the day with the help of Juliet's Nurse. This lively fifty-minute one-act comedy sparkles with wit and an in-depth understanding of the characters of these indelible ladies, and their effects on playgoers over the centuries. (Cameo appearance by Shakespeare at the end is optional).

BAKER'S
PLAYS

Baker's Play
7611 Sunset Blvd
Los Angeles, CA 9004
Phone: 323-876-057
Fax: 323-876-548

BAKERSPLAYS.COM

MURDER AT THE GREY'S HOUND MANSION
Maxine Holmgren

Mystery, High School/ Community Theatre / 5f, 3m */ Simple Set*
This is a mysterious comedy (or a comical mystery) that will have
everyone howling with laughter.

The eccentric owner of Grey's Hound Mansion has been murdered. The cast gathers at the gloomy mansion for the reading
of the will. Lightning lights up the stage as thunder and barking
dogs greet the wacky characters that arrive. Each one is a suspect,
and each one suspects another. Mixed metaphors and allitera-
tions will have the audience barking up the wrong tree until the
mystery is solved.

Baker's Plays
7611 Sunset Blvd.
Los Angeles, CA 90046
Phone: 323-876-0579
Fax: 323-876-5482

BAKERSPLAYS.COM

STONE SOUP
Anne Glasner & Betty Hollinger

Musical, TYA/Children's Theatre / 9m, 7f, 2 either / Simple Set
2 hungry soldiers stumble on a town filled with disgruntled
neighbors. Using their imaginations, the soldiers trick the townsfolk into donating seasonings for their legendary Stone Soup,
which they have convinced the townsfolk is a delicacy beyond
measure. They con the townfolk into giving them all the ingre-
dients to make a real soup, and in doing so, the soldiers help
the townsfolk learn how to get along with each other by working
together to create something good.

Baker's Play
7611 Sunset Blvd
Los Angeles, CA 9004
Phone: 323-876-057
Fax: 323-876-548

BAKERSPLAYS.COM

ELEANOR FOR PRESIDENT
Merritt Ierley

18+ m, 9+ f, ensemble (some gender flexibility and doubling possible)
A woman as Chief Executive? The 2008 presidential campaign proved it possible, yet it just might have happened more than half a century earlier. Eleanor Roosevelt, First Lady from 1933 to 1945, might have run for president after the death of her husband, Franklin. Many thought about it, some talked about it, a few actually suggested it. That Eleanor Roosevelt did not seek public office was of her own choosing, and chiefly her own priorities as well as a sense that the time was not yet right. Act I of Eleanor for President briefly scans her career to a point where she might have run. Act II fictionalizes the fork in the road not takes. The net result is a unique, sometimes witty, and always insightful look at Eleanor Roosevelt and the political process.

BAKER'S
PLAYS

Baker's Plays
7611 Sunset Blvd.
Los Angeles, CA 90046
Phone: 323-876-0579
Fax: 323-876-5482

BAKERSPLAYS.COM

Lightning Source UK Ltd.
Milton Keynes UK
UKHW051930140220
358759UK00005B/204

9 780874 409505